Grange Hill Graffiti

PHIL REDMOND

Grange Hill Graffiti

Based on the BBC Television Series
GRANGE HILL
by Phil Redmond

A Magnet Book

For A, E and A
My very own G-Team

First published 1986 as a Magnet paperback
by Methuen Children's Books Ltd
11 New Fetter Lane, London EC4P 4EE
Text copyright and TV format © Philip Redmond 1986
Cover photographs copyright © BBC Enterprises 1986

Printed in Great Britain
by Richard Clay (The Chaucer Press) Ltd,
Bungay, Suffolk

ISBN 0 416 64650 6

ONE

'IZ ZIG A PIG?' There it was in 300 millimetre letters scrawled in blue chalk. It formed the bottom half of a circle so it looked like it was smiling down at him. Underneath someone else had written 'YIZ HE IZ!' Below that someone had added 'IZ HE PIGZIG ABOUT IT?' Ziggy took a look around. Naturally there was no one to be seen right then, but someone had put it there. He had a fair idea who it was. Imelda Davies. He turned away and headed for the canteen. He'd come back later and scribble over the graffiti. Right now he wanted to concentrate on how to get back at Imelda. The feud was on again.

Ziggy shared the same feelings as most of the pupils at Grange Hill. When Danny Kendall from Form S3 had thought up the 'Speaking Wall', everyone had said it was a great idea. Ziggy had agreed. Somewhere you could go and officially scribble, draw, spray or write anything about anyone at any time. It *was* a great idea, so long as the graffiti was done by you, and not about you. Ziggy remembered how Stinko Stanley had burst into tears and run out of the school when he saw what someone had written about him. Ziggy had never seen what it was because the staff got old Griffiths, the school caretaker, to paint over it. Everyone knew Stinko stank. No one knew why. No one sat next to him. No one mentioned it. Until Kendall's Speaking Wall appeared. Since then, Stinko hadn't been back to the school. Don't blame him either, Ziggy thought, as he went through the door towards the canteen. I feel bad enough now, being picked on in front of the whole school. And it didn't say much about me. If someone wrote something really nasty it'd be terrible. He turned and looked back through the window at the Speaking Wall. A gang of first years were in a huddle, sniggering away at some of the words they'd only just learned. I'll really sort out Davies this time, Ziggy thought as he turned into the toilets. Or perhaps it isn't her. Perhaps it's that Kendall bloke I should sort out. That stupid wall was his idea, wasn't it? Bit of a headcase himself he is, so I've heard. Always bunking off and that. Soft clown. Yeah, but it was Imelda Davies who put it there, wasn't it? It's her I've got to sort out.

Ziggy washed his hands, then had to dry them on the back of his trousers because all the paper towels had gone – as usual. He left the toilet and headed towards the canteen. He thought back to how the feud had begun. He had clashed with the school witch on his first day. She had been frightening some girl with a frog. He had stopped her. Later, when he was trying to put the frog back in the school fountain she had attacked him, so he had pushed her in too. She had asked for it – and got it. Unfortunately, she had got her own back in a particularly nasty way by stuffing fibreglass down his back. That had kept him off school for a week and led to his incredible journey to Liverpool.

Ziggy still smiled when he thought back. Sneaking on to a shuttle jet trip to Manchester. Being collected by his sister Allison. He'd been well and truly sorted out by his mum when he was sent home the next day, but it had all been worth it. He had been lonely and wanted to see his two sisters who had had to stay in

6

Liverpool when he, his mum and his dad had moved south so that his dad could get a job.

He didn't feel lonely at Grange Hill any more. Apart from his arch enemy, Imelda, he had also made a few friends, especially Robbie Wright, a boy in his form. Together they made up the G-Team. They had tried a couple of times to get Imelda, but it had always ended in failure. The worst attempt was when they tried to bomb her with a giant balloon filled with water. It had proved so heavy that when they tried to lift it, it had rolled back and burst all over them. Somehow, Imelda lived a charmed life. But it won't last, thought Ziggy, as he spotted Robbie saving a place for him in the queue.

'Where've you been?' Robbie asked.

'Taking a pike at the Speaking Wall,' Ziggy replied.

'A what?' Robbie asked, rather puzzled. He still wasn't used to Ziggy's Liverpool accent, or his slang.

'A pike,' Ziggy repeated. Then added in response to Robbie's blank stare, 'A blimp. A scan? Casting me bins over it? Flippin' 'eck, Robbie. Haven't you heard of nothing?'

'Nothing like that I haven't,' Robbie confirmed.

'I was er . . . taking a look at the Speaking Wall.'

'Oh . . . well why didn't you just say so then?'

'I did, didn't I?' Ziggy protested.

'No,' said Robbie, firmly. 'Anyway, was it any good?'

'Nah,' Ziggy said, 'same as this morning.' Ziggy hoped Robbie hadn't seen it.

'Oh . . .' said Robbie, rather nonchalantly. 'Nothing to be "Pigzig" about then?' he asked.

Ziggy grinned. He should have known Robbie would see it. 'Nah,' he replied once again. 'Not as

7

much as Davies is going to have to be pig sick about!'

'Oh no,' groaned Robbie. 'Not again, Zig.' He'd obviously not forgotten the drenching he got from the giant balloon. 'Can't you just write something about her on the wall?'

'Yeah,' nodded Ziggy as they shuffled up the queue. 'Like, which hospital people should send flowers to.'

Robbie rolled his eyes, moved forward and collected his lunch from the dinner lady. He turned and started to look for an empty place as he heard Ziggy reach the serving counter. 'Is that all I get?' Ziggy was asking.

'Yes,' replied the dinner lady.

'Isn't there anything else I can have?' Ziggy protested.

'Oh yeah,' said the dinner lady. 'The back of my hand if you don't move.'

Robbie was still laughing as they sat down at a third year table.

'This is a third year table, you know.' said a voice from the other end of the table.

Robbie looked up to see a spotty bloke in glasses glaring at them. He looked across to Ziggy, slightly unsure about what do to. Ziggy wasn't. 'That's OK,' Ziggy announced, as he sat down. 'There's no need for you to move somewhere else. We don't mind sharing, do we, Rob? You just carry on . . . and . . . er . . . could you wack the salt down here, please?'

'I'll wack you in a minute,' the spotty bloke said.

'I said "please", didn't I?' Ziggy responded.

'And I said "push off".'

'Or what?' Ziggy shoved a sausage into his mouth.

'Or I'll push you off,' Spotty replied.

Ziggy shook his head and tutted loudly, 'There's

8

so much violence in the world today, isn't there, Rob?'

Robbie didn't say anything. He just carried on with his lunch. He didn't want any of the world's violence coming near him.

The spotty bloke went to stand up, but a girl sitting opposite put a hand across and stopped him. 'Leave him alone, Mike. There's nowhere else for them to sit.'

Spotty sat down again. Ziggy leaned forward and saw that the girl's voice belonged to Laura Reagan. She was in Form S3 and had a mum who taught sport at the school. She was also, according to Ziggy, a cracker. He'd often stood and watched her walking across the playground or down the corridor. In a lot of ways she reminded him of his sister Allison. Nice legs. The long hair. Well, until Allie got hers cut short.

Ziggy winked at Laura. She smiled back but turned to talk to her friend, Julia Glover. Spotty glared at Ziggy. Ziggy was going to wink at him, but knew he had pushed him too far already. He decided it would be better if he concentrated his efforts on clearing the rest of his chips from his plate. Wonder if Spotty's her boyfriend, he thought. Nah. She looks too good to go out with a wreck like him. Mind you. Look at our Allie and Dopey Dennis. He's a waste of space, isn't he?

He took another look at Laura as she stood up with Julia, picked up her plate and took it back to the serving hatch. Although Ziggy watched her until she had disappeared round the corner in the corridor, she didn't look back. Ah well, he sighed. At least she smiled at me. And at least she didn't walk out with spotty-features there. His eyes went back along the table to find Spotty polishing off his rhubarb crumble and custard.

Spotty stood up, took a long, hard look at Ziggy, and then said, 'Next time, find your own table!'

'Yes, sir!' Ziggy announced, through a mouthful of mashed chips and beans.

The third-former took one more look at Ziggy, which was enough to warn Ziggy not to push it any further, then left.

Robbie let out a sigh of relief, 'You're crazy, you are! What'd you have to wind him up like that for?'

'He asked for it.'

'So did you.' Robbie stood up. 'Do you want some puddin'?'

'Is the Pope a Catholic?' Ziggy replied. 'And see if there's any seconds.'

Robbie rolled his eyes once again and set off for the serving hatch. Ziggy set about his last sausage and about how to get back at Imelda Davies.

TWO

While Ziggy's mind started to compute ways of getting back at the evil Imelda, the other female he had just been thinking about turned the corner outside the school library. Laura Reagan was on her way to another meeting of SPEC, the Staff Pupil Editorial Committee for the school magazine. Behind Laura was Julia Glover, who was moaning about having to leave behind her pudding.

'It's full of sugar, anyway,' Laura responded. 'Besides, I thought you were on a diet.'

'I said I was thinking of going on a diet,' Julia moaned.

'Oh yes?' asked Laura. 'Which one? The old "see-food" diet. See food and eat it?'

'I love apple crumble.'

'That's all right then,' replied Laura. 'It was rhubarb!'

'I don't care. I'd prefer that to going to another of these boring things.'

'That's the way the pudding crumbles, kid,' Laura laughed.

'Have you ever thought of becoming a comedienne?'

'No.'

'Good. I'd hate you to be disappointed,' Julia said as they reached the door to the library. 'Do we have to go today? Couldn't we go down to the precinct and get my ears done?'

'You won't. We've been four times already. You'd just chicken out again.'

'I wouldn't. Not today. I've been thinking about it,' Julia insisted.

'You always are. But you never do anything about it,' Laura responded dismissively.

Laura was right. Julia had been thinking about it. Ever since the night of the "all-nighter", when she and Laura had been caught. She had been trying to pluck up the courage to disobey her father once again.

Julia had always had problems with her father, but at the moment it was almost unbearable. He watched her like a hawk. He wanted to know every little detail of where she was going. What she was doing. Who with. At what time. She knew the present problem was her own fault for trying to deceive him. The first time was when she and Laura had gone to St Saviour's Jumble Sale instead of the Library. He had caught them then as well. The most recent was when they tried to go to an all-night party. She and Laura had said they were going to stay with Laura's father, but had been found out. Her mother had realised that she had taken a sweater she was supposed to leave behind. Her parents had then gone round to Laura's and it soon became obvious that Laura had also lied to her mother.

That was the worst part, the fact that she had got Laura into trouble. Julia often thought about it. Laura had a great relationship with her mother. They really got on well. Laura had told Julia that it was because they only had each other, so took more care of each other. Made a greater effort to get on. Julia knew what Laura meant, but she also knew there was more to it than that. Laura's mum treated her as a friend as well as a mother. She didn't treat her like a little girl, like Julia's father did. What had really upset

Julia at the time, and still bothered her, was that she had jeopardised that relationship. Because she desperately wanted to go to the all-night party, Laura had lied to her mother. She had broken the trust that had existed between them. Although Mrs Reagan had been fantastic over the whole thing, she was still annoyed and upset at Laura for lying. She had even told Laura she would be unable to trust her word in the future, even though Laura promised it would never happen again.

All these things flashed through Julia's mind as they passed through the doors into the library and headed towards one of the tutor rooms at the back. If Laura was prepared to do that for me, she thought, the least I can do is sit through another of these boring meetings. She turned to Laura and said, 'Yeah . . . I suppose you're right. Perhaps I'll get my ears pierced on Saturday.'

'Some chance,' Laura threw over her shoulder as she found a seat near the front. They were, as usual, first there. The room was empty, but Laura liked to be at the front. She liked to be where the real discussion and decisions took place. Laura wasn't a follower. She was a leader. She loved to get involved in anything like SPEC.

She was a bit of a crusader.

It was Laura who had played a major role in launching the school's anti-smoking campaign. It was a topic that Laura was almost fanatical about. She detested smoking and would never miss an opportunity to have a go at anyone who was 'polluting her atmosphere'. She was always reminding everyone of the dangers, and facts like that at the age of 13, 20% of girls smoke; while tobacco advertising is banned on television, the tobacco companies get

13

about 300 hours of exposure, or really an hour a day, through their sponsorship of sport. She could be a right pain at times, grinned Julia. Especially to Danny Kendall. Kendall was the undisputed President of the Smokers' Union at Grange Hill. He stank of tobacco and Laura never let him forget it. It didn't seem to bother him though. He just ignored her, like he did everyone else. He was in a world of his own, was Danny Kendall. He'd have to be to come up with the idea of the Speaking Wall, Julia thought, as she stood looking out of the library window. A sixth former was spraying something on to the wall, but stopped as old Griffiths, the caretaker, came past. Griffiths hated the wall. Julia could almost feel his sense of outrage as he walked past and deliberately avoided looking at it. He pretended it didn't really exist. Organised vandalism, was how Julia had heard him sum it up. I suppose he's right, she thought, as she moved away to sit next to Laura. More like controlled vandalism though, she thought, as she sat down. She was preparing herself to doze off when the meeting began, but was pulled back to full consciousness when Laura suddenly spoke.

'I hate your dad. Do you know that?'

'Er, no . . . I'm not surprised but, er . . . why? Why say it now?' Julia asked.

'This.' Laura held up the latest edition of the school magazine. 'The way he put a stop to us including a league table of how our no-smokers were doing!' The table Laura referred to had shown how those people who had given up smoking were doing. The idea behind it was that if you made the information public it would encourage those who had given up to keep it up. It had worked well until Julia's father, in his role as a school governor, had protested that it actually

14

encouraged smoking. No one could really figure out his logic. Especially as he, himself, was a non-smoker. Laura still had difficulty. Julia didn't bother. She knew it was impossible.

Mr Glover had said that if you accepted that people were smoking, by encouraging them to give up, it was breaking the school rules which said no one should smoke. If anyone entered the no-smoking competition they had to admit they were smoking, so would therefore be admitting that they were breaking the school rules. As a result they should be punished. If they weren't, the staff were acting irresponsibly by failing to enforce the school rules.

Julia, like Laura and many others, had tried to convince her dad that that wasn't the point. They were trying to stop people killing themselves by helping them to stop smoking. That was the real problem. People find it very hard to stop. For the scheme to work it had to be allowed to break the rules. Laura had even shouted at him that they were trying to save lives not school rules, but he wouldn't listen. Rules are rules are rules are rules. That was his only response. Like a robot. In the end the scheme had collapsed. Julia nodded at Laura, she knew what she meant. 'I know,' she said. 'And you want to try living with him.'

'No fear,' Laura replied. 'It's bad enough seeing him when we go to your house.'

Julia just nodded. She didn't want to continue the conversation. They'd had it so often before. She had no need to worry. Just at that moment Miss Partridge came in with Calley Donnington of Form E2, Fay Lucas of N5 and Mr King, the Computer teacher. Julia nudged Laura and nodded at Fay as she found a seat next to Mr King. 'Never too far apart, are they?'

'You what?' Laura asked.

'You must have read it,' Julia said.

'Read what?'

'The Speaking Wall.'

'About those two?' Laura asked.

'Yeah. I'll show you after.'

Laura looked at her friend. For the first time that day she had a smile on her face. It was more of a grin than a smile. But it intrigued Laura. For the first time she wanted the SPEC meeting to hurry up and end. She wanted to know more about Fay Lucas and Mr King.

THREE

Ziggy was beginning his third bowl of rhubarb crumble. Robbie was beginning to feel sick watching him polish it off. Julia was dozing through the SPEC meeting and Laura was watching Fay and Mr King with great interest. Down by the canal a bottle was bobbing about in the water, doing its best to avoid a series of stones being thrown at it from the bank. The bottle was not at great risk as the stone-thrower was not really trying too hard. It was just something to do. Something to let out frustration.

Anthony 'Ant' Jones had a lot to be frustrated about. He had a continuing feud going on with one of the school's toughest and least-flexible teachers, Mr Bronson, his Form Tutor. He also had a girlfriend who was still living in fear of the dreaded Imelda Davies. Every time they made arrangements to meet anywhere outside school, Ant was never sure that Georgina would turn up. Like now. Ant was throwing stones at the bottle because Georgina Hayes was late.

Ant threw his twenty-third stone and missed again. Enough's enough, he thought to himself, about both the bottle and Georgina. If she can't be bothered to come, why should I hang around for her? He picked up one final stone and was about to throw it when a voice called from behind, 'Don't smash it!'

He turned to see it was Georgina. Her hair falling over her face as usual. She looked great. At least, she did to Ant. His irritation about her lateness started to ebb away as soon as he saw her.

'Not much chance of that, Gee.' He threw the stone to prove the point. It missed. The bottle bobbed away a bit further. 'And I've had plenty of practice,' Ant added, unable to keep some irritation out of his voice.

'Oh ... I'm sorry,' Georgina said, as she moved across and touched his hand. 'I got held up.'

'Who by? Or do I need to guess?' he asked. Georgina turned away. It was enough of an answer for Ant. 'Imelda Davies?'

Georgina nodded.

'Why don't you tell someone about it, Gee?'

Georgina liked him calling her Gee. He had only just started doing it but she felt as though it was something special. As though they were getting closer to each other. She turned back to face him. 'You know why.'

Ant did. They had talked about it often enough in the past. Georgina had once been one of Imelda Davies' gang. They called themselves the Terrorhawks, after some television programme Georgina had never seen. The three Terrorhawks of Grange Hill had been Imelda, Georgina and another girl called Helen Kelly. It was really Helen who was Georgina's friend – they lived near each other – but then Helen had made friends with Imelda. Georgina had known them both at primary school, and had admitted to Ant that she had been involved in some of Imelda's earlier escapades at Grange Hill, but only when they had been for a bit of fun. She had broken the odd light, or sprayed the odd slogan before the Speaking Wall was invented. It was only when Imelda appeared to go crazy and start hurting people that she decided to break off their friendship.

It was the fibreglass down Ziggy Greaves' back that

18

had started her thinking. This was followed by Imelda trying to introduce a protection racket on the first years. Georgina had wanted nothing to do with any of that. When she met Ant at the school Disco Club she decided to ditch Imelda. Unfortunately, Imelda was not an easy person to ditch. She had immediately accused Georgina of grassing on her, and only Ant saved her from being beaten up by Imelda and Helen.

Imelda was then suspended for a time, but vowed she would get even with Georgina. There was nothing to get even about, but Georgina took the threat seriously. She knew Imelda. If she believed something, no matter how ridiculous it was, then that was it – that was the gospel. Unfortunately for Georgina, the gospel at the moment was that Imelda still 'owed her one'. As a result of all this, Georgina very often found herself a prisoner in the school during break and lunch hour. She had to stay within sight of the staff or out of Imelda's way. The first was the easiest to do, even if it was inconvenient.

'What happened this time?' Ant asked as he flopped down on the old railing that ran along the edge of the canal.

'She was hanging about the main gate. I had to go out through the one they use for the kitchen deliveries,' Georgina explained.

'It can't go on like this, you know.'

'I know, I know.' Georgina stood up and started to walk down the canal.

'I'm sorry, Gee.' He put his arm round her shoulders. 'I know she's a real problem.'

Georgina felt a little uncomfortable, out in broad daylight like this, but it felt good. Ant's arms were strong. His shoulder was firm. She felt safe when he

19

was around. 'I wish you could be with me all the time,' she said.

'So do I.' He then laughed, 'I could always beat her to pulp, if you like.'

'Hhmm. That would solve one problem,' Georgina said. 'But wouldn't help with your Bronson problem all that much, would it?'

'Guess not,' Ant replied.

'And you can't always be there, can you? It's OK when we meet in school, but when you're not there, or I have to go somewhere to meet. . . .' Her voice trailed off. A thought had suddenly hit her. Why had Ant asked her to meet him here? Why not in school? She looked up at him. He was watching something on the far bank of the canal. 'Have you been in today?' Georgina asked. It was a casual remark. At least, it was meant to sound casual. It was also meant to catch him out. It did. He hesitated and flustered a bit before he answered.

'Er . . . er . . . yeah. Course I have,' Ant replied.

Georgina stopped walking, letting his arm fall from her shoulders. 'You haven't, have you?' she asked. He didn't answer, but turned and looked out across the canal. He had been watching a well-dressed woman throwing a bag of rubbish into the water. She then turned and walked away.

'Funny, isn't it?' Ant said, nodding across at the woman. I bet she'd go spare if we threw a sweet wrapper in her garden. But she comes down here and dumps her rubbish in the canal. If it sinks, you can't see it, so it doesn't matter!'

'Don't try and change the subject,' Georgina said. 'You haven't been into school today, have you?'

'No. So what?'

'So what?! You've got enough problems as it is.'

20

Ant just shrugged. 'Bronson thinks I'm a dead-head, doesn't he? Might as well act like one.'

'But you're not. You know you're not,' Georgina said firmly.

'What's the difference if you are or not? It only matters what they think, doesn't it? They decide how you're going to be treated. How we're going to get on in life. If he believes I'm trouble, I'm trouble, aren't I?'

'But there's no sense in proving it for him, is there?' Georgina asked.

Ant still didn't respond. His problems with Bronson had been going on all year. It was just a clash of personalities. The two didn't like or understand each other. Because of it, every time something happened between them it tended to blow up into a major conflict. Ant couldn't really remember how it all started, but it grew into a major problem when, ironically enough, Ant stepped in to save Georgina from Imelda.

After that brief skirmish, Imelda was dragged away and Ant stayed to comfort the shaken Georgina. Bronson had discovered them having a kiss and a cuddle and practically attacked Ant. He had struggled and caused Bronson's wig to fall off.

At any other time this may have been funny, but because the two were already at loggerheads, the incident was blown out of all proportion. Bronson accused Ant of assault.

Mrs McCluskey, the Deputy Head, asked Ant to apologise, but he wouldn't because he thought Bronson had attacked him first. The situation escalated to the point where Ant was facing suspension. It was only when Georgina threatened not to see him again unless he apologised, that Ant was persuaded he couldn't win. He apologised. That situation blew over, but it further deepened the rift between Bronson and Ant.

The latest clash was when Bronson found Ant sticking a notice up in one of the school's new portakabins. Because Ant was using drawing pins, Bronson went through the roof about the holes in the wall. He started to rant and rave about 'it being further evidence of Ant's wanton vandalism'. Bronson had accused him of being a persistent trouble-maker. He had called Ant insolent and arrogant. Georgina had been as amazed as Ant. Even Mr Baxter, whom Bronson had called in, felt it was more of a misunderstanding than wilful damage. Ant had got away with a warning about changing his attitude to Bronson, but didn't know how he could. The man didn't like him, and he didn't like Bronson. They would never got on together. Ant knew this, so did Georgina. They also both knew that because Bronson was the teacher he was bound to win. Ant was right. Whatever Bronson thought, would happen. What could they do to prevent it?

'Well, we can stop giving him all the evidence he needs, for a start,' Georgina said in reply to Ant. 'What good will it do staying off school?'

'What good will it do going to school?' Ant replied, with a touch of sarcasm in his voice. 'He'll only pick on me again, won't he?'

'Not if you keep out of his way, he won't.'

'How can I? He's my bloody Form Tutor, isn't he? The only way to keep out of his way is not go in. Which I am doing. Starting today.'

Having said that, he turned and walked off up the canal. Georgina didn't follow. 'And do what you despise me for, you mean?'

22

Ant stopped. 'You what? I don't despise you for anything.'

'Yes you do. The way I run away from Imelda.'

'It's a bit different, isn't it?'

'Is it? We're both running away from bullies, aren't we?'

Ant stood and thought about it for a moment. Then he walked across and put his arms around Georgina. As he did he remembered doing it once before and Bronson catching them. He grinned.

'Can't see what you've got to grin at,' Georgina said.

'No, but Bronson won't catch us here, will he?'

She smiled. 'Will you come back to school? Please. For me?'

'Will you tell someone about Imelda?' Ant replied.

Georgina looked down. She wouldn't answer. She couldn't. She was too afraid. Ant knew this. He pulled her closer to him and made two decisions. The first was that Georgina was right; he was stupid to stay off school. It did give Bronson more ammunition to use against him. The second was that he was fed up seeing Georgina so frightened of Imelda. He would sort that out. By sorting out Imelda – once and for all.

FOUR

By the time Georgina and Ant had walked back to school, Ziggy was lying on top of the bike sheds recovering from his mammoth intake of rhubarb crumble. Robbie was still recovering from watching the disgusting event. The SPEC meeting was drawing to a close and Laura and Julia were dashing down to the Speaking Wall. They needn't have bothered. Old Griffiths had decided the wall was too much to live with. He had decided to give it a coat of paint.

Everyone had agreed that the wall should be painted over when it was full, or at least each week, to provide a fresh wall to write on. Whereas everyone else assumed that 'once a week' meant every seven days, Mr Griffiths decided that 'once a week' meant once each week. If that meant a Friday one week, a Wednesday the next, a Monday the next, then that didn't matter. Slogans might only last four days instead of seven but so much the better. The wall was an eyesore. No one had consulted him about it. No one else had volunteered to paint it. So he would do it. But when he felt like it. Like now.

'Oh no,' groaned Laura, as she and Julia came to a sliding stop by the wall. She turned to Julia. 'What did it say about Fay? You've got to tell me now.'

'I don't know,' Julia said.

'What do you mean? You acted as though you did upstairs.'

'I know. I was only trying to impress you. Sorry. Mike just mentioned it to me over lunch.'

Laura looked around. She had the scent of gossip now. She had watched Fay and Mr King all through the meeting but hadn't detected that anything was going on. But, if there was, if a fifth year girl was going out with one of the teachers, she wanted to know. 'Where's Mike now?' she suddenly asked.

'How . . . how should I know?' Julia demanded.

'Let's go and find out. C'mon.' Laura grabbed Julia's arm and practically dragged her away towards the general teaching block. As she did, she also nearly kicked over Mr Griffiths' tin of paint.

'Oi. . . .' He scowled. 'Watch it! I don't care if your mother is a teacher or not.'

'That's good,' called Laura over her shoulder, as they sped off in search of gossip. 'Neither do I!'

It took a moment for Mr Griffiths to realise that what Laura had said could be classified as impertinence, but before he did, she was gone. He tutted to himself and shook his head. At least the wall was repainted. He put the lid back on the paint tin and walked away.

Although Ziggy and Robbie were watching Mr Griffiths from the top of the bike sheds, neither of them could see the smirk on his face as he sauntered away. Everyone had agreed that the wall should be painted. So painted it was. Everyone had agreed it should be painted white. So painted white it was. But no one had agreed on what sort of paint to use. So old Griffiths used his own. They would all find out soon enough.

'He's a nut-job that bloke,' Ziggy announced. 'He's only supposed to paint that bleedin' wall once a week.'

'Or when it's got too much on,' Robbie reminded him.

'Yeah, but he's never got his paintbrush out of his hand, has he? It's always bleedin' well full.'

Robbie just shrugged. He wasn't bothered either way. He'd never written on the wall. And never had anything written about him. Not like Ziggy. 'Anyway, I'd have thought you'd have been glad. You wouldn't be Pigzig, like?' he asked.

'Yeah. But . . . well, there's somethin' funny going on there.'

'How d'you mean?' Robbie asked as he kicked a pebble off the roof on to a first year. The two roof-dwellers jumped back as the first year looked up to see where the pebble had come from.

'Well, when that other headcase invented the wall. . . .'

'Who? Danny Kendall?' Robbie interrupted.

'Yeah. When he first invented it, hardly anyone used it.'

'Probably frigtened in case anyone saw what they were writing,' Robbie suggested.

'Yeah. Probably,' agreed Ziggy. 'But now it's full-up in two days. Then painted over by Groucho Griffiths before anyone gets a chance to see it.'

'So?'

'So. I don't know!' replied Ziggy. 'Just doesn't seem right, that's all.'

'Neither do a lot of things. Especially her.' Robbie nodded across the playground. Ziggy followed Robbie's eyes to see Imelda coming round the corner of the Science Block. She had Helen Kelly in tow and they looked like they were hunting. Hunting for trouble.

Ziggy watched her for a moment, then turned to Robbie. 'You still got any of those big balloons left?'

'Yeah. . . .' He looked across at Imelda.

27

'What do you reckon?' Ziggy asked.

Robbie just nodded. Then asked, 'When?'

Ziggy pushed up Robbie's sleeve. Nearly half-past one. 'Better make it tonight. After school.'

Robbie just nodded again. 'Where?'

Ziggy turned, lowered himself on to his stomach, eased himself backwards, over the edge of the bike shed and dropped to the ground. 'Wherever she is!' he called back up to Robbie. 'C'mon. Let's go and mess up old Griffiths' nice clean wall.'

He turned and walked away. Robbie waited for a moment. He wanted to make sure Imelda was well and truly gone. Girl or no girl, she was, as Ziggy had so often called her, a right nut-job. You only tangled with her when you had either no choice, or the element of surprise. Robbie watched her go off towards the general teaching block. He lowered himself on to his stomach, edged over the side and dropped to the floor. Ziggy was right. Tonight would be the time to take Imelda.

FIVE

Totally unconnected with any of the day's previous events, the former moles of Grange Hill, Luke 'Gonch' Gardner and Paul 'Hollo' Holloway, had embarked on a new career. They had sat quietly and eaten their packed lunches, completely undisturbed by the usual chaos and mayhem of the lunch break. They had been able to watch all the comings and goings around the Speaking Wall without anyone bothering them. They had watched Imelda write about Ziggy. They had watched Ziggy read it. They had watched old Griffiths paint it. They had watched Laura and Julia just miss it. They had even been able to watch Ziggy and Robbie climb up and down from the bike shed roof. They had been able to enjoy all this in an atmosphere of peace and quiet because of their new careers as steeplejacks. They were lying on the roof of the general teaching block.

It had been Gonch's idea. It always was. His natural curiosity, as he called it. Nose bigger than his brain, Hollo called it. As well as stupid. He called it that too. Like the time Gonch had had his Walkman confiscated for the second time. To avoid getting into aggro with his mum he had come up with the idea of breaking into the school to get it back. Naturally, Hollo had gone with him. Someone had to look after him, Hollo would argue. They had got in through the boiler house and along the ducts that carried the central heating pipes. Which was how they had become moles. They had managed to get the Walkman back, but also managed to set off the burglar alarm.

When Hollo thought back he couldn't believe they had got away with it. He couldn't believe their luck had held out so long. But it had. Which was probably why he now found himself lying on the edge of the general teaching block roof looking down at Ziggy Greaves climbing off the bike shed roof. If he and Gonch had succeeded in breaking into the school, surely they'd manage this. That's what he kept telling himself. But, somehow, he wasn't too sure.

It had all started that morning in History. Neither he nor Gonch liked History. That wasn't too unusual in itself, he couldn't think of anyone who did. Except, of course, Swot Hunter. Swot liked everything. Except PE. There were no books or homework to do for PE. So he never brought his kit. So he had to go to the library to do extra work. Still, he seemed happy. At least, he didn't seem unhappy. He just always seemed the same. A swot's a swot, I suppose, thought Hollo. Wonder if he ever gets excited about anything? Never seems to. Probably hasn't even got a telly at home, never mind a video. Probably wouldn't even see it if he did. Thickness of those glasses he wears. Wonder if that's why he is a swot. His eyes are so bad he can't see to do anything else. Couldn't exactly play footy with those specs on, could he? Or swim, or bomb about the gym. Yeah. That's it. That's probably why he always gets away with it too. If me or Gonch forget our kit, it's a quick belt with the slipper and an undies and shirt job. Never happens to Swot though.

Hollo grinned. He was pleased with this piece of reasoning and turned to tell Gonch. 'Hey, you know Swot Hunter?'

'Yeah. What about him?' asked Gonch.

'I reckon I know why he never does games,' Hollo said. 'He's got something wrong with him.'

'Yeah,' said Gonch. 'Got a hole in his heart or something, hasn't he?'

'Has he?' Hollo asked, in total shock.

'Yeah, something like that. He has to go for regular check-ups at the hospital. Has special pills as well.'

'Oh ...' said Hollo. His own theory sounding rather ridiculous now. 'How'd you ... er ... how'd you know that?'

'I asked him,' replied Gonch.

'Why?'

Gonch shrugged. 'Wanted to know how he got away with not doing PE all the time. So he told me. Why, anyway?'

'Oh ... er ... nothing. I was just thinking about him.'

'Oh ... do you do that often?' Gonch asked. Then added with a grin. 'I'll have to stick something about you on the Speaking Wall down there when Griffiths has finished painting it.'

Hollo didn't bother to reply. He shook his head. Poor old Swot. Hollo never realised he was that bad. He then began to wonder why he was thinking about Swot. Then he remembered. History. He and Gonch had been doing their best to amuse themselves until the end of the period by seeing how far a one centimetre ball of paper would go if it was flicked up a copy of 'An Introduction to English History' held at an angle of approximately sixty degrees. The furthest they'd got was the back of Calley Donnington's head, when Gonch spotted the workman.

He was standing on the roof of the general teaching block. They couldn't see what he was doing but he was walking around prodding the roof with some-

31

thing. Hollo had asked Gonch what he thought it was. Gonch reckoned it looked like one of those metal detectors you saw wallys wandering around the parks with on Sunday mornings. It did, but it probably wasn't.

After about fifteen minutes the workman disappeared from in front of their eyes, but an idea appeared at the back of Gonch's brain. To get on to the roof.

What would it be like on top of the school building? How would they get up? There must be a way. How else had the workman got there? They'd go and find out at lunch time. It was just natural curiosity.

It was also bloomin' stupid, as Hollo pointed out, but he had gone with Gonch. They had sat down during Art and drawn out a rough plan of the general teaching block. They put in all the corridors, stairways and doors that they could remember. They then compared the plan with the building at lunch time. The first thing they discovered was how many doors they had missed off. They realised that they had remembered, and therefore included on the plan, only the doors that they used or passed regularly. There were lots they had overlooked. Of course, most of these were locked. One door wasn't, but it was only a cleaner's storeroom. Gonch found a brand new pair of rubber gloves and a new mop-head he thought might come in handy for something – perhaps as a spare wig for Mr Bronson. Hollo had agreed they might come in handy. Especially for the cleaners, who would also probably go beserk if they were missing. Gonch agreed. Left the mop-head, but couldn't resist the rubber gloves. They had too many possibilities for a laugh.

Eventually they had found another unlocked door

and discovered it was a stairway up into a kind of hut built on to the roof of the building. Inside the hut was a large water-tank that fed all the cold water for the sinks and toilets. Gonch knew about tanks because they had had to have a new one at home last winter. The old one had sprung a leak. Gonch remembered it well because it had happened in the middle of the night. The tank was in the loft over his bedroom. In fact, right over his bed. And he had been in bed at the time!

When they got into the tank room, they discovered a small hatch that opened out on to the roof. This was obviously how the workman had got there. It was also how Gonch and Hollo got out and discovered the peace and tranquility in which to eat their lunch.

The only thing they hadn't been able to figure out was what the workman was doing on the roof. That is, until they stood up to begin their descent.

'Come on,' said Gonch. 'We'd better get down before the lunch break finishes. The workies have probably only gone for theirs.' He stood up and headed back towards the hatch in the side of the tank room. He didn't get far. He had only taken about six steps when he heard a loud crack and a cry behind him. He spun round just in time to see Hollo disappear in front of his eyes. One moment he was there, the next he was gone, and the only sign that he had ever been there was a screwed up crisp packet. It was lying on the roof next to a large hole. Gonch edged forward. He could see Hollo lying about ten feet below him. He wasn't moving.

SIX

If Ant and Georgina had looked up at the roof of the general teaching block as they came into school, they could have seen Gonch standing, staring down at something. They didn't because their eyes were looking in the opposite direction. They both appeared to be studying each other's feet as they approached the main gate in subdued silence. They hadn't spoken since they had left the canal. Suddenly the silence was broken by Georgina. 'Why does life have to be like this?'

'How do you mean?' Ant replied.

'Complicated. Nothing's ever easy, is it?'

'It could be,' Ant said. Then smiled. 'If we just did what everyone else wanted us to do. And not what we wanted to do.' He took hold of her hand. 'Like this.'

'Don't,' Georgina said, slightly embarrassed, pulling her hand away. 'Someone might see us.' Ant grinned. 'It's kissing they put you in front of the firing squad for, not holding hands.'

'I'm not taking the risk,' Georgina told him quite firmly.

'Sorry,' Ant said.

Georgina smiled. They walked a few more paces before she spoke. 'What'll you say at registration. Where will you say you've been?'

Ant shrugged. 'Dentist?'

Georgina rolled her eyes. 'Everyone says they've been to the dentist. The whole school should have no

35

teeth left by now. Besides which, they ask to see the appointment card now, don't they?'

'Yeah. I think so,' Ant nodded. 'I'll just say I didn't feel too good this morning. Which is almost right, isn't it? I didn't feel up to seeing Bronson.'

'Won't Bronson ask for a note?'

'Oh yeah. But I'll tell him I'll get it tomorrow because my mum wasn't in. Which is also true. She went off to order some new furniture or something this morning.'

'Will he accept that?' Georgina asked, sounding slightly worried.

'Probably not,' Ant replied. 'But he won't have much choice this time. He'll have to wait until tomorrow. And then I'll have my note.' He grinned, 'Even if I have to write it myself.'

They reached the door to the general teaching block. Georgina stopped. 'He knows your writing,' she pointed out. 'I'll write it for you.'

'Deal,' said Ant.

'OK,' said Georgina. 'See you after?'

'Of course. Main gate?'

'Yeah. See you later then.' Georgina turned into the block, expecting Ant to carry on walking. However, he didn't. He nipped in after her, pulled her under the stairs and gave her a quick kiss. Then dashed away.

'Tony!' she called, half protesting, half giggling. 'What was that for?'

'Making me come back in today,' Ant shouted. 'You're right. I'm not going to give Bronson the proof he needs. See you later.' Georgina stood and watched him go off across the playground towards a group of people gathered around the Speaking Wall. She was waiting for him to turn so she could wave. However, before he did she spotted something out of the corner of her eye: Imelda. She was coming towards her from the main gate. She hadn't seen Georgina yet, so Georgina turned and raced upstairs to registration, hoping their form tutor was already there.

As she turned away, Ant also turned back to wave. He saw her go, sensing something was wrong. It didn't take him long to figure out what when he saw Imelda and her sidekick, Helen, come into view. For a moment Ant didn't know what to do for the best. He wanted to go back, to make sure that Georgina was safe, but he also wanted to get to registration ahead of Bronson. That was difficult enough in itself as Bronson always got there ahead of the first warning buzzer. He always did so nobody had an excuse for being late. Ant had to be there before him. Especially as Bronson would be gunning for him for being absent that morning.

Reluctantly he decided to go on to registration. It was what Georgina wanted, and he knew she'd be able to look after herself inside the school. All she had to do was keep close to the staff.

He walked past the group standing near the Speaking Wall, pausing once again to look back towards the door where he'd left Georgina. He'd toyed with the idea of writing something on the wall. The equivalent of carving something on a tree – a huge heart with their initials inside. But now he wasn't in that kind of mood – he was in the mood for sorting out Imelda Davies. He wasn't going to have her worry Georgina any more. By the end of the day he'd see to that.

SEVEN

As Ant made his way to registration and thought about how he would deal with Imelda, he had no idea that he would have to join a queue. He would have to stand in line behind someone he had just passed at the Speaking Wall. That someone was of course Ziggy. Standing with him was Robbie. They were both watching Calley Donnington's face as she tried to write something on the wall.

'It won't stay on,' Calley announced.

'You've said that about fifty times now,' Ziggy chipped in. 'And tried to write it about twenty.'

'Well, what's wrong with it?' she turned and asked Ziggy.

'Dunno,' he shrugged. 'Looks like old Groucho Griffiths has used some kind of special paint. See. It's still wet.' He poked the wall with his finger, the end of which turned white.

Calley leaned forward to examine the wall. 'Is it just wet?' she asked.

'Yeah,' Robbie answered.

'Nah, it's more than that though,' Ziggy added. 'It's like some kind of jelly, isn't it?'

Calley prodded it with her finger. 'Urgghh. It's all sticky and slimy.' She tried to flick the blob of paint off the end of her finger, but it wouldn't go. She tried to make the blob stick back on to the wall. It wouldn't. In the end she bent down and ran her finger along the ground to scrape it off. Then she stood up and tried once again to use her marker pen. No good.

It didn't even leave a mark. She then took out a piece of chalk. That didn't work either. It was like trying to write on jelly. 'It just ... it just seems to absorb everything,' Calley announced.

Ziggy raised his eyes. 'Don't start again.'

'Well, he shouldn't have done this, should he?' she protested. 'The SPEC meeting agreed to put up a notice about the school Fun Run. It should go on the wall. It's supposed to be the way we communicate with each other.'

Ziggy threw a look at Robbie, then spoke, 'I know that. You know that. So does everyone in the school. Including old Groucho Griffiths. But he hates this wall, doesn't he? So, he's trying to put the mockers on it, isn't he?'

'Put the what on it?' Calley asked. 'Is that the sort of paint he's used?'

'Nah, bubble brain. He's trying to knacker it. Use this special paint so we can't write on it.' Ziggy looked at Robbie and raised his eyes again.

'Is he, now?' Calley said. 'Well, we'll soon see about that.' She hurried off in the direction of the Caretaker's room, to find Mr Griffiths and ask him what he was going to do about it.

'What do you reckon it is, Zig?' Robbie asked as he climbed up the ladder Mr Griffiths had left by the wall, and fingered the paint.

'Anti-burglar paint,' Ziggy announced with confidence.

'You what?'

'I saw it back home in Liverpool. They used it at me last school. It's a special kind of paint that they use on drain pipes and roofs and that. You know. It doesn't dry, so burglers and robbers can't climb up it.'

'Sounds like a good idea,' Robbie said.

'Yeah. But not for walls we're supposed to write on,' Ziggy commented. 'He's a crafty old so-and-so old Groucho, isn't he?'

'You can say that again,' said Robbie.

'He's a crafty old so-and-so old. . . .' Ziggy started to say it again, but stopped when Robbie kicked him. He laughed. 'Only trouble is though, where do we write our invitation to that headcase Imelda?'

'Don't know,' Robbie said as he jumped off the ladder. 'We could always pass her a note in registration,' he suggested.

'Nah,' Ziggy said. 'It won't have the same impact as a direct challenge on here. For all the school to see.'

'Well you're not going to get that today, are you?' Robbie pointed out.

'Doesn't look like it,' Ziggy agreed. 'Come on then.' He turned away. 'It looks like it's just going to have to be the old-fashioned method.'

'What's that?'

'A good smack in the mouth!' Ziggy announced as he headed off towards registration. 'Are you sure you've still got one of those balloons?'

'Yeah . . . look,' Robbie answered, holding up one of them.

'Right then. Challenge or no challenge, she's going to get it at half-three this savvy. OK?'

'OK!'

They walked off totally unaware that at half-three, Ant Jones would also be looking for Imelda.

They were also unaware that, as they walked into the general teaching block, Gonch was still hovering above the hole in the roof, three floors above them.

EIGHT

Hollo moved. At last, Hollo moved. First an arm. Then a leg. He was alive. Gonch closed his eyes and blew out a long sigh of relief. He felt like he'd been lying on the edge of the hole, staring down at Hollo, for hours. It was probably only minutes. It was almost a lifetime.

When Hollo had disappeared, Gonch had edged forward to peer into the hole. The whole roof seemed to have caved in and Hollo was lying among the debris. Gonch had called out to him over and over, but had got no response. Just as he was starting to panic, starting to worry that Hollo was seriously injured or even dead, Hollo's arm moved.

The wave of relief that swept over Gonch felt as warm as sunshine. 'Hollo,' he called for about the hundredth time. 'Hollo, are you all right?'

'Orraaghhh,' was the only response.

'Hollo. Speak to me. Are you all right?'

'Oh yeah . . .' Hollo moaned. 'I'm great. Never felt better!'

Gonch grinned. Hollo was all right.

'What . . . what happened?' Hollo asked as he opened his eyes and blinked against the daylight shining through the hole in the roof.

'You fell through the roof,' Gonch told him.

'How?'

'How should I know? Must have been rotten or something. Probably what that workie was doing up here this morning.'

'Yeah . . . ooowww,' Hollo exclaimed as he rolled on to his side to get up.

'What's up?' Gonch asked, slightly panicky in case Hollo had broken his arm or something.

'Sat on a nail. It's all right. I'm fine now. Just get me out of here.' Hollo demanded.

'Are you sure? Waggle all your legs and fingers and things.'

'What?'

'Waggle everything about,' Gonch insisted. 'Make sure it's all still working.'

'It's all working enough to strangle you when I get out of here,' Hollo hissed at Gonch.

'I'd better leave you in there then, hadn't I?' Gonch countered.

'Just get me out, clown!'

Gonch looked around. He couldn't see anything to lower down to Hollo so he could climb out. 'Isn't there any way out down there?' he asked.

Hollo looked round. His first impression was of being in a totally square box. As his eyes adjusted to the light he could see he was in a small room about half the size of the stockrooms they had off some of the classrooms. He noticed that the room was not, as he first thought, square but was more of an oblong. It was about two metres long and about 1.5 metres wide. Hollo also noticed that only three of the four walls were plastered and painted. The fourth, one of the narrow ones, was made of rough brickwork, as though it had been added later. Something else Hollo realised, with a feeling of mounting panic, was that there was no door. This room had, for some reason or other, been bricked up. There was no way out except through the hole in the roof. That was three metres above him and way out of his reach.

'See anthing?' Gonch called.

'Only disaster,' Hollo replied, sinking to his knees.

'Isn't there a door or something?'

'No. I'm completely walled in. Probably forever too, knowing you,' Hollo moaned.

'I'll get you out.'

'How?'

'I don't know yet. But have I ever let you down before?' Gonch asked, totally seriously.

Hollo could have reeled off at least twenty instances where Gonch had led them into disaster, but he didn't. What was the point? Gonch would never accept it anyway. So long as they got away with it in the end, Gonch dismissed it. To Gonch, Hollo thought, disaster was being caught. You could rip your pants. Lose all your worldly possessions. Be late for school or whatever. But, so long as you didn't get caught doing it, it was fine. No problem. A good laugh. Yeah. This is hilarious, isn't it? He looked up at Gonch. 'What are you going to do?' he asked.

'I'll, er . . . I'll go and see if I can find something to get you out,' Gonch replied as he stood up.

'What about old Griffiths? He'll get me out,' Hollo suggested.

'And he'd turn us in. No. I'll go and see what I can do. I won't be long.'

Hollo was going to say something, but he didn't get the chance. Gonch had gone. Blast, Hollo thought. Why me? Why does it always happen to me? They're his crazy ideas but I'm always the one who ends up like this. Like when we went down the central heating ducts. It was my pants that got ruined by that oily water. Never him. Well, this is it. If I get out of this one, that's it for me. I've retired from the natural curiosity and nosey parkers' club. From now

45

on I'm staying on the ground. Not over it or even beneath it. Right there. On the ground.

Having made that decision he settled down to wait for Gonch's return. There was nothing else for him to do.

Gonch went across the roof, in through the hatch of the tank room, down the stairs and out into the general teaching block at just below the speed of sound. He went along the corridor and down the stairs, four at a time. He was heading for the boiler room, or more correctly, the Caretaker's Store that was right next to it. He had decided half-way down the stairs from the tank room, that what he needed was a ladder. He knew that Mr Griffiths kept his ladders there.

As Gonch came round the corner of the school kitchens, he slowed down. If he was seen running it would attract too much attention. He had to be careful to act normally, not draw attention to himself. He wasn't really supposed to be there. If he got stopped he would say he was looking for the Care-taker. However, he needn't have worried as no one stopped him and no one saw him.

He tried the door to the Caretaker's Store. It opened. Inside, on clips on the wall, was a ladder. It was the only one there so Gonch grabbed it and ran. It was made of aluminium, so it was quite light. He made good progress back to the general teaching block. He was even able to get all the way back to the tank room, before he hit a problem. He couldn't get the ladder round the huge water tank and out through the small hatch on the roof.

He stood back to survey the problem. The main obstacle was that the hatch was below the top of the tank. To get the ladder through the hatch would mean having, somehow or other, to push it across the top of the tank, then lift one end so it tipped over the edge, slid down and out through the hatch.

As he lifted the ladder on to the top of the tank he managed a grin. Spud Murphy, the Maths teacher, would have had a mathematical equation or something to work this out. Perhaps I'll ask him what it could be, Gonch thought. But sometime in the future!

He slid the ladder across the tank. It's lucky this is made of aluminium, Gonch thought, or I'd never have been able to do this and . . . Oh no! Blast. Damn! Bloody hell! He stood back and stared at the tank. The ladder had fallen in. Right in. Gonch had thought the ladder would go right across the huge tank. It hadn't. It had fallen into the water. It was now lying on the bottom. Gonch stood and stared. What was he going to do now? How would he fish it out? There was nothing nearby. He considered dashing off to find something and was about to start down the stairs again when the first warning buzzer sounded for the start of the afternoon lessons. Registration would begin in five minutes.

Oh no, groaned Gonch. I've got to get Hollo out now or we'll be missing from registration. He took another look at the ladder resting on the bottom of the tank. He knew there was only one thing to do. With a huge sigh, he quickly stripped off all his clothes and edged himself into the tank. 'Aargghh . . . it's freezing,' he muttered to himself. 'Aagghh . . . God . . . I hope no one comes up here now. Getting caught is one thing. Getting caught in the flesh is something else.'

The water must have been about a metre deep, as it came up to his waist. He didn't fancy ducking under so he tried to fish the ladder out with his feet. As he

47

did he could feel little bits of rust and rubbish moving about beneath his feet. He remembered his dad telling him about how you can often find dead birds in these tanks. They fly in for a drink, fall in and drown. He hoped he wouldn't stand on one. He also reminded himself never to drink from the school hot or cold taps ever again. He'd only use the taps marked 'Drinking Water'.

He hooked a foot under the ladder, lifted it up and managed to grab it with his hands. Oooaagghh! The cold water lapped up over his shoulder. Still, he had the ladder. He lifted it up over the side of the tank. Angled it down toward the hatch and pushed. It slid out on to the roof.

Gonch was pleased. At least that bit worked. Then he froze. Something touched his leg. Was there something living in the tank? He didn't wait to find out. He was out of the tank in one leap. He looked back but couldn't see anything as the water was now very murky and rust-coloured. He'd definitely remember never to drink it.

He used his underpants to dry himself. He reasoned that although he might be in for an uncomfortable afternoon, his undies would be the least obvious article of clothing to have missing. The underpants were no substitute for a real towel, so, by the time he was dressed again and lowering the ladder down to Hollo, he was still a bit soggy.

'Where've you been?' Hollo asked impatiently.

'Having a swim,' Gonch replied.

'What?'

'Never mind. Grab the end of that,' Gonch said as he lowered the ladder.

Hollo did so. As the ladder disappeared into the hole Gonch had to bend forward. Just as he had misjudged the size of the tank, Gonch had misjudged the length of the ladder. It was too short. If only he had taken Spud Murphy more seriously!

Hollo looked horrified as the ladder slid through the hole and fell against one of the walls. He pulled it upright. It was a full metre too short. Even if he leaned it against the wall and climbed to the top, he couldn't reach the hole. He was still trapped.

'What now, dimple head?' he shouted, more angry than worried that Gonch had messed it up.

As he spoke, the second buzzer sounded for registration. 'I'd better go to registration first,' Gonch said.

'What about me?'

'You've gone to the dentist,' replied Gonch.

'What?'

'That's what I'll tell them. Er . . . I know,' Gonch grinned, 'I'll say you suddenly found you had a hole and went to get it filled!'

'Very funny! Then what?'

'I'll get a bigger ladder.'

'Where from?' Hollo asked.

'I don't know yet. I'll think of something. Won't be long. I'll get my mark and then come straight back.' As Gonch moved off he dropped something down to Hollo. 'Hang on to that for me will you? Save me carrying them. With a bit of luck we'll be out and on time for English. OK?'

Hollo didn't get a chance to argue. Gonch was gone. He bent forward and picked up what his friend had thrown down, and saw it was Gonch's wet underpants. Instinctively Hollo dropped them on the floor. He had no idea where they'd been! He also had no idea how long Gonch would be. At that moment, neither had Gonch!

NINE

Ant arrived at the form room before Bronson. He sat at one of the front desks and made sure he was doing nothing that could be misinterpreted when his teacher arrived. He decided to concentrate on a book and resist the temptation to join in the conversation as more and more people arrived. He even made sure he was reading one of the set books. He didn't want to be doing anything that could antagonise Bronson.

Things weren't too bad, until Laura and Julia arrived. As soon as he heard Laura buttonhole Mike Sunderland about Fay Lucas and Mr King he had to turn and listen.

'Come on, Mike, you must have seen it,' Laura was saying. 'Julia said you told her over lunch.'

'You did, Mike,' Julia confirmed.

'I didn't really see it,' Mike said.

'God, this gets worse,' Laura moaned. 'Did you or didn't you?'

'No,' Mike answered.

'You told me you did,' Julia protested.

'Like you told me you did,' Laura pointed out.

'Danny Parkinson told me,' Mike offered. 'He's in N5. Fay Lucas's form,' he explained.

'Well, what did he say?' Laura asked. She still wanted as much gossip as she could get.

'Just what I told Julia. It said, er . . .''Do Fay and King Compute? Or are they FAYKING IT?'''

'That wasn't what you told me,' Julia protested. 'You said "Does FAYKING compute"!'

'It doesn't matter what the exact words were,' Laura announced. 'Now that we'll never see them. The interesting thing is, that someone is saying that there is something going on between them.'

'Yeah. . . . Do you think there is?' Julia asked.

Laura was about to answer, but she was interrupted by Mike. 'Er . . . have you finished interrogating me? Can I go now?'

'Oh er . . . yeah. Sorry, Mike,' Laura smiled at him. He didn't smile back as he went and found a seat at the back and took out a crumpled copy of NME to read.

'Well?' asked Julia, repeating her question. 'Do you think there is anything going on between Lucas and Mr King?'

'I do!' piped up a voice from near the door. They turned to see Louise Webb coming into the room. 'I've just seen them coming out of the Golden Swan together.'

'What?' asked Laura. 'The pub by the precinct?'

'Yeah. I had to pass it on the way back to school. Looked pretty cosy together too,' Louise added.

'This gets better,' Julia chipped in.

'It still doesn't really mean anything,' pointed out Laura. 'They could have been doing anything in there.'

'Yeah. Or the obvious,' added Louise.

'What do you think?' Julia asked Laura.

Laura shrugged. It sounded really interesting now but she couldn't say anything as Mr Bronson walked in. Immediately, silence descended over the room. People who were sitting on desks slid off them. People who were leaning on walls straightened up. People who were sitting stood up. Everyone came to attention. Not really out of respect, but out of fear. Everyone was on their guard.

No one was more on their guard than Ant. He had been listening attentively to Laura and the others. He was wondering if they talked and speculated about him and Georgina like this. Probably not, he thought. The gossip's more juicy if there's a teacher involved. He was just beginning to accept that he was actually interested in the gossip himself when everyone jumped to attention. He turned to the door to see Bronson standing there. Damn, he thought. I could have got caught out there.

Fortunately, he hadn't, as Bronson made his way across to the teacher's desk and put down the register with his usual precise manner. This is it, thought Ant. I'd better get out and speak to him first, before he gets to me on the register. If I leave it, he'll get the advantage. I'll have to see if I can get in first.

Ant stepped forward. He felt his throat tighten. His mouth was dry but his hands were wet with perspiration. 'Er . . . excuse me, sir,' he stammered.

'Ah . . . Jones. Decided to join us this afternoon have you?' Bronson's eyes practically burned into Ant's head. He was like an eagle, waiting to pounce on its prey.

'Er . . . yes . . . I mean, no, sir,' Ant responded. He cursed himself as he did, as he realised he had given Bronson an opening.

'Oh . . . haven't quite made up your mind?'

'No, sir, I mean, it's not that, sir,' Ant stopped. This was getting worse. He was so worried about making a mistake that he was falling over his own tongue.

'Then what is it, boy? Speak out!' Bronson roared.

Ant took a breath – it was now or never, 'I want to apologise for this morning, sir.'

'Do you now?'

'Yes, sir. I didn't feel too well. My mother wasn't able to give me a note today, but she will confirm it in writing tomorrow morning.'

'Your mother wasn't able?' Bronson enquired. He had spotted the flaw in the story and was preparing ready to pounce. 'And why wasn't she able? Can she not write?'

'Of course she can, sir.'

'I see. Then was she poorly herself? Were you struck down by a family ailment perhaps?'

'No, sir. She was – well, she wasn't there, sir.'

'She wasn't there?' Bronson asked. A slow smile breaking across his lips. 'Then if "she wasn't there, sir," how can she write a confirmation note tomorrow?'

Ant knew he'd spot it, but he had to press on, 'Because I'll tell her, sir.'

'I see. So, in other words, cutting across the corner, so to speak, I have to take your word for it.'

Ant could see where Bronson was leading him, so chose his words carefully, 'Er . . . no, sir. You have to trust that my mother would write an accurate note.'

Bronson nodded. 'But she can only write such a note based on what you tell her. She has to trust you. Does she not?'

God, it's like being on Crown Court, this, thought Ant. 'Er . . . yes, sir.'

'And if she has to trust you. That means I have to trust you. Trust *you*, Jones. Does it not?'

Ant knew Bronson wanted him to agree so he could pull out something from the past when Ant had lied to him or let him down. So Bronson could prove he couldn't trust him. Once again, he chose his words carefully, 'Er . . . you have to decide whether or not to accept my mother's note, sir. Whether or not you want to argue with her.'

Bronson did not respond. He stared at Ant for a moment or two. He was aware that the rest of the form were listening. Watching the game of verbal chess as Bronson tried to catch out Ant. He also knew that Ant had thought this out very carefully. He wasn't going to make a mistake now. Bronson decided to wait. There were always plenty of opportunities to catch out people like Jones. 'Very well,' he finally said. 'Let's wait for this note. First thing tomorrow morning. Without fail, Jones. Without fail.'

'Yes, sir. Thank you, sir.' Ant sat down as Bronson started the register. He found it very difficult to be civil to Bronson. He detested him. But he knew he had to do it to survive. He'd also promised Georgina. He only hoped now that he could convince his mum, or that Georgina could forge her handwriting.

Still, he felt sure he'd solved his short term problem with Bronson, although the long term problem still remained. All he had to do now was sort out Georgina's problem with Imelda. He would do that at 3.30 pm.

TEN

Just as Ant was narrowly avoiding his disaster with Bronson, Georgina was desperately trying to avoid one of her own.

Since she left Ant, she had been hiding in the toilets. Her form tutor had not arrived when she reached the form room, so she decided to try and hide until registration started. Being told off for being late was better than being early and beaten up by Imelda.

As she sat huddled on the pan, so her feet wouldn't show below the door, she began to realise how silly it was. Everyone hid in the toilets. She had been on more than enough hunting trips with Imelda to know that when people are being chased they usually make a dash for the toilets. They dive into one of the cubicles, lock the door and pull their feet off the floor hoping whoever it is will go away. It never worked when she helped Imelda chase people. It didn't work now.

Georgina screamed. There was a loud bang and the cubicle door flew open and crashed against the side. The next thing Georgina saw was Imelda's shoe, still in the position it had been when she kicked the door open. The next thing she heard was Imelda, using that tone of voice Georgina knew so well. When she sounded so friendly, Imelda was at her most dangerous. 'Well now, Georgie. So this is where you've been hiding is it?' Imelda grinned. 'We've missed you, you know. Haven't we, Helen?'

As she spoke, Imelda looked up and Georgina

followed that look to find Helen up above her, leaning over the wall of the next cubicle.

Taking her eyes off Imelda was exactly what Georgina knew she shouldn't do. But was exactly what Imelda wanted. No sooner had Georgina looked away than Imelda had jumped forward and grabbed her by the hair. Two great handfuls. She twisted her fingers into Georgina's hair and tugged. There was no way Georgina could now pull free. She had to go where Imelda dragged her. Which, for the moment, was out of the cubicle and towards the row of sinks on the wall near the door.

'You've been spending too much time with that poncey third year, Georgie. You seem to have forgotten all your old mates,' Imelda shouted as she shoved Georgina towards one of the sinks. 'Get the tap, Helen.'

'No ... stop it. Please, Imelda,' Georgina pleaded.

'Don't worry, Georgie. We're not going to hurt you. . . .' Imelda laughed. 'We're only going to help you wash your hair.'

Georgina could see Helen turning on the taps in the sink. For some strange reason the water was a horrible brown colour. Like mud or rust.

'Don't, don't please,' Georgina continued to plead.

'Why? We all like to keep our hair clean, don't we?' Imelda laughed again. She tried to force Georgina's head into the rapidly filling sink. Georgina resisted by putting her hands on the front of it. Imelda nodded to Helen, who grabbed Georgina's arms and tugged them away. Imelda now twisted her hair.

'Oowww. Please ... you're hurting me,' Georgina cried.

'No I'm not. You're hurting yourself by struggling,' Imelda shouted down Georgina's ear. '*This* is me hurting you!' As she spoke she punched Georgina in the back. The blow winded Georgina but it gave her an opportunity to pull free – in order to punch her Imelda had loosened the grip on her hair. Georgina twisted away, although she lost a tuft of hair between Imelda's fingers.

'Come here!' Imelda screamed as Georgina backed away across the toilets. 'Come here I said,' Imelda screamed again.

'Why? Why are you doing this?' Georgina screamed back.

'Because I don't like people who grass on me, that's why!' Imelda smiled. Almost calm.

'I didn't grass on you. Honestly I didn't,' Georgina insisted. 'I didn't, Imelda. I just don't want to go around with you any more, that's all.'

'Oh. That's all, is it? Too good for us now are you? Now that you've got that poncey boyfriend?' Imelda turned to Helen. 'What's his name, Helen? Worm? Or slug, or something, isn't it?'

'He's an Ant!' Helen said with a sneer.

'Oh yeah. Whoever heard of anyone going out with an Ant?' Imelda exchanged another grin with Helen. She was hoping Georgina would take her eyes off her again. But Georgina had made that mistake once. She wouldn't do it a second time. She continued to back away from Imelda until she hit the wall of the toilets and could go no further. She knew it would happen any moment now. Imelda would wait and then make a leap at her. She wanted to take a quick look around to see if she could find either a way out, or something to fight with, but she knew that would be fatal. It would give Imelda exactly the opportunity she wanted. Georgina was well and truly trapped. Oh, where was Ant now, she thought.

Imelda edged herself back on her heels, ready to spring forward. She turned to Helen to give her the signal to move, but just as she was about to pounce, she was stopped dead by a loud knock on the door and the bellow of a familiar voice. 'Anyone in there?' It was Mr Griffiths.

Imelda automatically turned to see what was happening. Georgina seized her chance, shoved Helen at Imelda and dashed past and out of the door, nearly colliding with Griffiths on the way out.

'Careful, Careful!!' Griffiths shouted. He then turned back, bumping straight into Imelda and Helen. 'Just a minute, you two. What's going on?'

'Nothing,' Helen answered, automatically.

'Think I was born yesterday?'

Imelda just looked at him but said nothing. All she was interested in was going after Georgina. She went to walk away, but Griffiths stopped her. 'I haven't finished with you yet,' he said.

She turned and looked at him.

'Well?' he asked her.

'Well what?' she asked him.

'What was going on just now?'

'Nothing. Can I go to registration now, please? I don't want to be late.'

Griffiths looked at her. He'd been around long enough to know when he was on to a lost cause. Imelda was definitely a lost cause. 'Anyone else in there?' he asked.

'No,' answered Helen.

He poked his head round the door. There didn't look like any damage, so he turned to Imelda, 'Go on then. Hop it!'

Almost before he'd got the words out, she was gone. Griffiths shook his head, then turned to Calley as he went into the toilet, 'Now then. What's all this about rusty water?'

Calley followed him in. 'It's not just the water I wanted to complain about. What about this sticky, gooey paint you've put on the Speaking Wall?'

'Sticky, gooey paint? . . . Oh dear . . . That's terrible. Deary, deary me!' he suddenly exclaimed.

'What!'

'It's terrible,' he announced.

'I know,' Calley agreed. 'And as a member of SPEC I want to complain about the fact that the Speaking Wall is supposed to be painted regularly so we can. . . .' However, she didn't finish. She didn't get the chance to finish.

'No . . . no . . . no,' he interrupted. 'Not the paint. The water!'

She looked to see that it was still running a horrible brown colour. 'That's what I told you,' she groaned.

'I know. And I'd better get to the bottom of this. I'd better get up to that tank room and take a look. God knows what I'll find up there.'

With that he turned off the tap and rushed out of the door, leaving Calley still slowly fuming about the state of the Speaking Wall. Well, she thought, if he isn't interested in it, I am. And if he's not going to do anything about it, I will. First she had to go to registration, but straight after she would go and find Laura Reagan. She'd know what to do.

ELEVEN

Gonch was beginning to believe that he was about to experience a disaster of his own. He hovered near the form room door. As soon as Miss Washington had called his name he slid out. He knew where he could get another ladder to free Hollo. He had seen it as he dashed across to registration. It was another one of old Griffiths' and it was propped against the Speaking Wall. If he could get that on to the roof he'd soon have Hollo out.

As he dashed down the corridor he kept looking back. No one called after him. Miss Washington didn't yell his name. He turned the corner. He had got away. He now had about seven minutes before English. Seven minutes to free Hollo.

As Gonch sped across the playground, he didn't realise that someone *had* noticed him sliding out of registration. Fortunately it wasn't Miss Washington, but Ziggy Greaves. Ziggy watched from the window of their form room as Gonch struggled to lower the heavy wooden ladder and started to drag it away. He had to find out what this was all about. He thought about telling Robbie but as his name was Wright it was one of the last to be called out. He decided to go alone.

Following Gonch's example, Ziggy edged over to and out of the door. Good job Miss Washington was leaning on the front row of desks instead of the teacher's desk.

Ziggy had covered the distance from the form room

to where Gonch was now trying to pull the ladder through the door into the general teaching block, in less than a minute.

'What are you up to?' he asked.

'Minding my own business,' Gonch replied.

'Are you? What is it?' Ziggy asked, nodding at the ladder. 'A window cleaning business?'

'Shouldn't you be in English?' Gonch said dismissively, trying to haul the ladder up the stairs.

'So should you,' Ziggy replied. 'And you'll never do it dragging that thing behind you. What's it for?'

'Never mind.'

'Come on . . . you might as well tell us,' Ziggy said. ' 'Cos if you don't you'll never get that upstairs on your todd. And then the bubble'll go in when registration finishes. You'll get sussed. Then I'll know. And you'll be in dead lumber. Right?'

Gonch stopped to consider the thought. Like Robbie, he sometimes found it difficult to follow Ziggy's slang, but he worked out that if he didn't do something quickly registration would finish and he would be found half-way up the stairs with old Griffiths' ladder.

He made an instant decision. 'Come on then. Give me a hand to get this up to the top and I'll tell you what it's about.'

'Tell me first,' Ziggy demanded.

'I haven't got time. Hollo's stuck. I need to get him out. Like – now! You'll see for yourself anyway, won't you?' Gonch insisted.

Ziggy nodded. That was true. 'OK,' he said. 'Come 'ead. Let's do it then. Where?'

'Right to the top!' Gonch announced.

'It would be, wouldn't it?' Ziggy moaned.

'You wanted to know!'

True, Ziggy thought, as he lifted one end of the ladder and they started to stagger up the stairs. Even with the two of them it was an effort to get the huge ladder up to the top. Fortunately they managed it without being seen or interrupted.

'So, what now?' Ziggy asked as they arrived. He could see no sign of trouble or need for a ladder.

'The end of the corridor. That door on the left,' Gonch replied.

'Why?'

'Just do it,' Gonch called.

Ziggy was going to argue, but the buzzer suddenly sounded. End of registration. Gonch dropped the ladder. Partly with fright, but partly in panic. What would they do now? Already people were spilling out of their form rooms to change over for the next period.

'The bogs!' Ziggy shouted and pointed to the nearby toilets. He then shoved Gonch forward and they crashed through the door, abandoning the ladder until changeover was finished.

Nobody paid too much attention to it. A ladder was a ladder. A few members of staff looked at it a bit strangely. It was left at a peculiar angle. Mr Bronson even walked past it, although he did make two third year boys straighten it up. Perhaps the staff were aware that there were workmen in the school. For whatever reason, when Ziggy and Gonch poked their heads out of the toilet door, all was quiet.

By now Gonch had told Ziggy what had happened and Ziggy was keen to help. He was even keener to find the way up on to the roof. Deciding that the time was right to make another attempt, they dashed out of the toilets, grabbed the ladder and hurried down the corridor towards the tank room.

As they reached it, they saw the door was ajar. 'That's strange,' said Gonch.

'What is?' asked Ziggy.

'I could have sworn I closed this door properly when I left.'

'Perhaps you didn't. Hurry up. This is heavy you know,' Ziggy urged.

'No . . .' Gonch muttered. He was still thinking about the door. 'I definitely closed it. So it wouldn't attract attention while I was gone. Someone's been here.'

'Or Hollo's got out,' Ziggy offered.

'No . . . he couldn't. We tried.'

'Well, we can't hang about here all day, can we?'

Gonch looked at Ziggy. He was right. They started up the stairs to the tank room. They'd only gone about three steps when Gonch stopped dead, causing the ladder to bang into Ziggy's chest.

'Watch it!' Ziggy protested.

'Ssshhh!' Gonch urged. He could hear voices upstairs.

'What's up?' Ziggy whispered, picking up the urgency in Gonch's tone.

'There's someone up there!' Gonch whispered back, straining his ears to pick up the mumbled voices. He leaned forward to catch the strains of the conversation, and as he listened he began to recognise one of the voices. It was old Griffiths! 'Quick. Out. Quick. Quick!'

Ziggy didn't need any further explanation. He could recognise panic at 100 metres. He pulled the ladder back with such force that he nearly pulled Gonch down the stairs. They turned back towards the toilets, dropping the ladder back in place by the wall as they passed.

'What . . . what was going on?' Ziggy asked as they dived into one of the cubicles and locked the door.

'I couldn't . . . I couldn't get it all . . .' spluttered Gonch, as he fought to regain his breath. 'Something about the state of the water.'

'What?' Ziggy asked. 'What about it?'

'I was, er . . . before I went to registration . . . oh . . . never mind. They just came up to examine the tank because someone had complained that the water was a funny colour,' Gonch said. He didn't want to go through the whole story about the other ladder and the tank. He felt stupid enough as it was, without letting Ziggy know about it.

'How long do you reckon they'll be?' Ziggy asked.

'I think they were about to go. We'll give them a couple of minutes. Then check. OK?'

'OK,' Ziggy nodded, then added, 'What time do you think it is?'

'Dunno. But I think we're late for English,' replied Gonch.

Several minutes later they were later still for English as they poked their heads out of the toilet door.

'Looks quiet,' Ziggy said.

'Yeah. . . . One of us needs to go and have a look. See if it's clear,' Gonch replied.

'And I know which one of us it should be,' said Ziggy. 'I'll wait here for you!'

Gonch knew he was right. It was really his problem. He stepped out and walked along to the door of the tank room. When he got there he received another shock. Old Griffiths had gone. But the door was locked.

Gonch couldn't believe it. He tried the door several times. He tried pushing it and pulling it in case he had just forgotten which way it opened. He hadn't. It was definitely locked. Hollo was trapped in a room with no door. There was only one way out and that was through the roof. Now they couldn't get to that roof. Now there was no way to get to him. No way, that is, unless they went to the staff and confessed everything. They might get Hollo out, but they would really be in trouble. Even to Gonch, this was beginning to look like a real disaster.

Ziggy was surprised to see Gonch coming back. He was even more surprised when he went past and down the stairs. 'What's up?' he called after him.

'The door's locked,' Gonch replied.

'So, where are you going?'

'English.'

'What for?'

'To figure out what to do next.'

Ziggy hesitated. It made some sense. They couldn't do anything here. So they might as well go there. Get their mark and hopefully come up with a solution. He ran down the stairs after Gonch.

TWELVE

Gonch and Ziggy were not the only ones who wanted to move quickly around the school after registration. The traffic between the first and third years was both fast and thick. Ant Jones hurried away from Bronson and S3 as fast as he could, with Bronson's final warning, about having the note from his mother available first thing in the morning, ringing in his ears. Ant was looking for Georgina. He wanted to make sure she was safe from the deadly Davies between each lesson changeover.

As Ant dashed one way, Calley Donnington was rushing in the opposite direction – from E2 to S3, to find Laura and Julia, her colleagues on SPEC. She was still annoyed about what Griffiths had done to the Speaking Wall. She wanted to tell them and try and enlist their help in trying to sort something out.

The Speaking Wall itself was well chosen being, as it was, in the centre of the school, and somewhere everyone had to pass. As both Calley and Ant did now. Neither had the time to notice Mr Griffiths. Neither of them had the time to notice the look of bewilderment on his face. His ladder. The one he had used to paint the wall. It was gone. He couldn't believe it. While he went to try and solve the mystery of the rusty water, someone had actually stolen his ladder!

Mr Griffiths looked one way. Then he looked the other. He saw Calley running towards the general teaching block and he saw Ant running towards the science block. He also saw a lot of the other 1198 pupils of Grange Hill milling about and going to and fro. What he couldn't see was the cat and mouse game being played out by a certain three of those 1198 pupils. The cat and mouse game that was going on in the second year cloakroom. The cat and mouse game that was going on between Georgina, Imelda and Helen. With Georgina as the mouse.

As soon as registration had finished, Georgina had dashed out of the room and off towards the English room. Imelda and Helen went after her immediately and to try and lose them Georgina ducked into the cloakroom and hid beneath a huge duffle coat. She was crouched on one of the benches, her back pressed against the wiremesh dividing partition. She was shaking and felt sure that Imelda would actually hear the wire shake.

Georgina heard the girls' footsteps getting closer and pulled the duffle coat tighter around her. 'Where is the little cow?' Imelda hissed at Helen.

'Don't know. She definitely came in here though. I'm sure she did,' Helen replied.

'Come on, Georgie!' Imelda suddenly shouted. It made Georgina jump. She wanted to cry, she was so frightened. She bit her lip to stop herself.

'We're going to get you so you might as well get it over with,' Imelda called. Oh why? Oh why? Oh why? Georgina asked herself. Why is she like this? Why can't she just leave me alone? She bit her lip harder as she saw Imelda's shoes through one of the sleeves of the duffle coat – she had it pulled so tightly that the sleeve stuck out like a tube. Imelda was standing right next to her. Georgina could feel the cold sweat on her back. If I'm holding this coat so tightly, she thought, will she notice? Will she find me?

70

'Can you see her?' Imelda asked Helen.

'No.'

'Cow!' Imelda cursed. 'Where is she?' Then Georgina's heart stopped beating. Imelda suddenly announced, 'Look under the coats. She'll be under one of the coats!'

Oh no, Georgina groaned to herself. She's bound to start with this one. She's bound to. She's standing right – aagghh. Georgina went rigid. She almost choked as her throat tightened and she stopped breathing. Imelda had pulled the coat next to her off its hook. Georgina's mind started to race. What'll I do? What'll I do? she thought. Shall I run for it? Shall I try and get away? Shall I . . .? She stopped herself. Made herself concentrate. Imelda hadn't tugged at the duffle coat. She had gone the other way. Georgina could hear the coats being pulled from the hooks as Imelda moved away from her. Georgina started to breathe again. But only for a moment as she realised that Imelda would be back. She would be working her way round the cloakroom. She may have started at the next coat to Georgina, but she would end up on the duffle coat that was, at the moment, protecting her.

What should I do? What should I do? Georgina started to panic again. Then she heard a familiar sound. The buzzer for the start of the first lesson of the afternoon. French. She heard Imelda's voice. 'Come on, Georgie. We know you're in here. We've got to go to French. So we might as well go together, mightn't we?'

Georgina didn't move. She suddenly realised she had one chance. French. French was next. She sat and waited. Eventually it was Helen who offered hope. She was speaking to Imelda but Georgina could

71

have hugged her. 'Er ... Meld ... let's go. It's Bronson next. You know what he's like.'

Georgina just listened. Imelda didn't answer. She could imagine her standing there. That fixed expression of hatred on her face. Especially if she thought she was being cheated of her prize.

Helen spoke again. This time more urgently. More insistent. 'Come on, Meld. Bronson will have us in detention if we're two seconds late. We can sort her out later. . . . Come on. She'll end up with detention anyway, won't she? Then we'll know where she is tomorrow night as well!'

It was obvious that this convinced Imelda. She suddenly laughed. 'Yeah. She gets a seeing to and detention! Yeah. I like that. . . . See ya', Georgie. See you in French!'

Georgina let out a long, slow, sigh as she heard Imelda and Helen go. To be sure, she stayed under the duffle coat for a few minutes. Then she very carefully and slowly looked out. They had gone. She gulped down a few lungfulls of fresh air, took a deep breath and looked at the duffle coat. She wondered whose it was. She would have liked to thank them for buying one so big. Then she jumped up and dashed out.

As Georgina ran down the corridor to the Language Lab she found Ant hovering outside. 'What are you doing here?' she asked.

'Came to see if you're all right,' he answered. 'I just saw the two beasts go in.'

'Is Bronson in there yet?'

'Er . . . yeah.'

'Damn!'

'Are you OK, Gee? Where've you been?' Ant asked, really concerned.

'I'm OK. I'll tell you later. I'll have to go.'

'Look. Wait here at the end of this. I'll come over. Walk you to your next class. OK?'

'OK.' She smiled and went into the room. Ant waited. He could see her through the glass in the door. Bronson seemed to be having a go at her for being late. He waited until she sat down, on the far side of the room from Imelda. Then he turned and hurried off. He was late himself.

Inside the room, Georgina saw Ant go. She smiled to herself. At least she had him in her life, even if she'd now lost an hour with him tomorrow night. She glanced across at Imelda, who was glaring at her. Still, at least an hour's detention is better than a beating up!

On the other side of the school, Calley had caught up with Laura and Julia just as they were going into their Home Economics group. 'Laura,' Calley called. 'Laura, can I see you for a moment?'

Laura stopped, slightly surprised to see it was Calley. 'Oh . . . hello, Calley. What's wrong?'

'You know at lunchtime, when we agreed to tell everyone about the school Fun Run. Especially the ex-smokers?' She knew that would catch Laura's attention. 'At the SPEC meeting,' she added quickly.

Laura exchanged a smile with Julia, then said, 'Er . . . yes. My memory can go back that far. What about it?'

'We said we'd put it on the Speaking Wall, didn't we?' Calley asked.

'Yes,' Laura answered. 'So?'

'Old Griffiths has painted it.'

'Yes. We saw it,' Laura said, now growing a little

impatient. She had to get in to Home Economics. Even if she didn't want to.

'Perhaps you did. But did you touch it?'

'Er ... no,' Laura admitted, looking to Julia, wondering if they had a basket case on their hands. 'No. I didn't.'

'It's some form of special paint. It's all sticky and gooey. You can't write on it.' Laura now became more and more interested as Calley explained about the non-drying paint and how she had tried to talk to Griffiths, but he was more interested in the colour of the water in the toilets.

'And it's definitely sticky, this stuff?' Laura finally asked.

'Yes,' confirmed Calley. 'I got a bit on my finger and had a terrible job getting rid of it. Why?'

'I don't know yet, but perhaps we could make use of that,' Laura said. She then turned to Julia. 'What's after this, Jules?'

'Er ... Computer Studies. With Fay Lucas's bloke.' Julia grinned.

'Who? Mr King?' Calley asked automatically.

Laura picked it up at once. 'What do you know about it?'

Calley shrugged. 'Only that they've been seeing a lot of each other. In and out of school.'

Laura smiled. 'There's got to be something in all these rumours,' she muttered.

'No smoke without fire?' Calley asked.

'Something like that,' Laura said. She then looked into the Home Economics group, now all seated. 'We'd better go. What have you got next, Calley?'

'Er ... English, Maths and then Library Studies,' Calley replied.

'Great,' Laura announced. 'In that case you can

74

get at the photocopier, can't you?'

'Er . . . yes. I think so.'

'Well then, can you knock up a leaflet about the Fun Run. And make about, ohh . . . I don't know, er . . . let's say two hundred copies?' Laura asked.

'Er . . . yes. I think I could do that as well,' replied Calley.

'Then do it.'

'Why?' asked Calley.

'Meet us by the Speaking Wall at 3.30 and I'll tell you then,' Laura said and turned away towards the classroom.

'What will we do with all those leaflets?' asked Julia as they found a couple of seats at the front of the room. Laura still liked to be at the front – even when she was late.

'I'll give you three guesses,' Laura said and took out her economics text books. Half an hour later, Julia had had nearly twenty guesses, and still hadn't come up with the right answer. But soon the whole school would know, never mind Mr Griffiths.

THIRTEEN

When Gonch and Ziggy abandoned the ladder once again and set off for English, Hollo began to feel that it was not only the ladder that was being abandoned. He looked at his watch. Twenty past two. What had happened to Gonch? He said he'd be back straight after registration. English had started by now.

He must have got into trouble, Hollo thought, as he picked up Gonch's wet undies once again. I wonder what did happen to these. No doubt he'll tell me, when he turns up. If he turns up. Yeah. Of course he will. He's not going to leave me here, is he? I mean, there'd have to be a good reason for him not coming back, wouldn't there? Old Griffiths being in the way or something. Yeah, that could be it. Griffiths was probably on the prowl. Could have even been down by that door, so Gonch is laying low. Waiting for him to go. Yeah. He'll be along in a minute. I hope.

Hollo was doing his best to remain optimistic, but with only the same four walls, the hole in the roof, the debris from that hole, the ladder and Gonch's wet undies, there wasn't much to give him hope. He sat down on one of the rungs of the ladder, now propped against the wall. I wonder what this place is anyway he thought. Looks like it's been like this for years. As though someone just decided to brick it up and not use it anymore. Seems like a bit of a waste of space to me. Especially as they're always wingeing on about not ever having enough. Hhhmmm. Wonder if they know it's here? Probably don't, do they? They'd use it if they did. Suddenly, another thought, an alarming thought, popped into his head. If no one knows it's here, and something happens to Gonch, what'll happen to me? No one would know I was here!

He began to think of all the things that could have happened to Gonch. He could have got blown off the roof, he thought. By a sudden gust of wind. He could have tripped inside the tank room and fallen into the tank. Banged his head and drowned. No, perhaps not. The sides of those tanks are too high. I know. He could have easily fallen down those stairs and bust his neck. It'd be dead easy that. Especially as he'd been hurrying. And he could have.... Stop it.... Stop it, he told himself. He could have done a hundred things. But he.... Then another thought occurred. What if he'd also fallen through the roof? What if he'd fallen into a room like this? With him trapped in there and me trapped in here. Neither of us would ever be found!!

Hollo sank lower on to the ladder. He fell forward and put his elbows on his knees. Come on, Gonch, where are you?

At that precise moment, Gonch was back in English. He had not fallen down any stairs, or through any holes in the roof. He and Ziggy were now facing a new danger. They had fallen into the hands of their English teacher, Mr Kennedy, second only to Mr Bronson for discipline and detention.

'Well?' Mr Kennedy was demanding. 'While I appreciate that it is hardly worth you gracing our presence with your company for what remains of the period, I, like everyone else, would be fascinated to hear what could possibly make you nearly twenty-five minutes late!'

'Er ... well, er ... you see, sir ...' Gonch started,

but not quickly or convincingly enough for Ziggy. Ziggy knew you had to be faster than that. Especially with the hardcases like Kennedy. You had to sound as though you meant it. He decided to take over.

'Nose bleed, sir,' he announced, with his usual confident tone.

'A nose bleed?' Kennedy asked. There was puzzlement in his voice. That was a good sign. Always keep them guessing was one of Ziggy's mottoes.

'Er . . . yes, sir. I get them every now and then,' Ziggy stated. Then added, 'Just happens. Wallop!'

'Wallop?' Kennedy queried.

'Yeah. Wallop. All over the show, like,' Ziggy heard a couple of the girls wince and draw breath at the thought of the nose bleed. Ziggy was convincing. That was good. That would help.

It seemed to, as Mr Kennedy was slowing down. 'All over the show?' he enquired.

'Yeah,' Ziggy pressed on. 'Usually knackers me kecks and all. But it never this time, like. Corker really.'

'Er, didn't it?' Mr Kennedy was beginning, like so many before him, to get lost in the intricacies of Ziggy's language.

'Nah. Gonch give us a hand see. Helped me suss it out and get me into the bogs smartish like. So he stopped it knackering me kecks and shirt and that.' Ziggy then smiled. That always helped. Mr Kennedy looked across to Gonch. Now totally lost. 'Is . . . is this true, Gardner?'

'Er . . . yes, sir,' Gonch confirmed. Then added, with just a hint of a smile, 'Just the way Ziggy described it, sir.'

'Right. As you've both obviously come through quite a traumatic experience I suggest you go and sit

79

down,' Mr Kennedy said as he motioned them to their seats. Ziggy and Gonch exchanged grins. They couldn't believe it. Kennedy letting them off. It was too good to be true. And it was. As they reached two empty seats at the back, Mr Kennedy dropped the bomb. 'You can also put your experience down on paper tomorrow night. One hour's detention. Each.'

Mr Kennedy turned back to the blackboard. Gonch and Ziggy turned to look at each other and Robbie turned to look at them both. He wanted to know what had really been going on. He took a quick look to see if Kennedy was watching and then mouthed the question to Ziggy, 'What's been happening?'

Ziggy just mouthed back, 'Tell you later,' then turned and exchanged a shrug with Gonch. 'It nearly worked,' he said.

Gonch nodded, 'One hour's not much. Considering how much detention Hollo's doing right now!' Ziggy nodded. Gonch turned his mind up towards Hollo somewhere above them. The English room was on the second floor of the general teaching block. The stairway to the tank room was on the top floor. Hollo had fallen down nearly four metres through the roof, which was about the same distance the staircase led up to the tank room. That meant he must be on the top floor somewhere. But where? Gonch drew a quick sketch of the building, trying to fill in all the details they had discovered during their earlier exercise at lunch break. He sat looking at it. He could work out where the tank room was in relation to the main stairwell, but no matter how hard he tried, he couldn't work out whereabouts Hollo was. He thought he had figured out where the hole was, but it didn't make sense. Unless, of course, Hollo had fallen straight into the Geography room. Obviously he hadn't. So where was he?

Someone else asking that same question, was Hollo himself. He had a sketch of the teaching block too – the one they had done that morning. He thought he should be in one of the rooms they used for Economics. But he wasn't. He put the sketch plan down and stood up. He looked up at the sky and the clouds passing overhead. Where was he? He didn't really care. What he really cared about was, where was Gonch? How much longer was he going to be? And the answer was, about an hour longer than Hollo expected.

FOURTEEN

At 3.25 Computer Studies came to an end with a discussion on the advantages and disadvantages of keeping hard copies. Everyone agreed a paper printout was desirable, despite the problems of storage and safety. Mr King had finished early because he wanted to get away to an appointment. 'Guess who with?' someone had shouted from the back, but Laura and Julia were now hurrying across to the library to join Calley Donnington to see how she got on printing the leaflets about the Fun Run.

Laura was in a bit of a temper because she had banged her leg on some 'stupid ladder' someone had left in the general teaching block. Worse still, she had holed her tights. Ugghh! Some people!

However, while Laura was angry and upset, Hollo was becoming more and more desperate as he stared up at the hole in the roof. He looked at his watch. 3.29. The buzzer should be going soon for the end of the school day. He had sat and listened to it go off six times through the afternoon. For registration and the beginning and end of the three afternoon periods. Well, for the first two periods. He was still waiting for the final buzzer. He was also still waiting for Gonch.

Where is he? Hollo wondered for about the millionth time. He said he'd be back in time to go to English. He should have well been here by now. Huh, knowing him he's probably decided to leave it till now. He'll get his mark and attend every lesson. It'll be me who'll have to do all the explaining tomorrow. I'll kill him when I get my hands on him, I really will. I'll kill him. He'll wish he could find a hole like this to hide in. Bloomin' nuisance. . . .

Hollo stopped thinking so he could concentrate on listening. There it was. The final buzzer of the afternoon. It was more of a low rumble than a buzz. He could hear the end of day commotion start. Doors opening and closing. The rush and thunder of feet as people made a dash for freedom. All the sounds were familiar. The noise of the changeover chaos. But the sound was muffled, as it came through the walls. Hollo had long since realised that as he had such difficulty hearing what he knew were quite loud noises, there would be very little chance of anyone hearing him calling for help. His only hope of getting out lay with Gonch.

He flopped back against the wall. Oh come on, Gonch. I won't really kill you. Not if you stick your head through that hole in . . . er . . . ten seconds. Ten. Nine. Eight. Seven. Six. Five. Four. Three. Two. One. And . . . nothing. Gonch didn't appear. Hollo had tried the trick at least a dozen times throughout the afternoon. But it hadn't worked. Where was he?

At that very moment Gonch was sticking his head between Ziggy's legs. It was not the sort of thing he'd normally choose to do, but by now they were all desperate enough to try anything. He was putting his head between Ziggy's legs so he could lift him up on his shoulders so Ziggy could peer in through the open window over the door of the Caretaker's room.

'Can you see anything?' Gonch asked.

'Yeah. They're on the hook on the wall. Hang on,' Ziggy responded. He then pulled himself up so he could stand on Gonch's shoulders. Gonch winced. This hadn't been part of the deal.

'Do you have to ... aagghh,' Gonch cried in pain as Ziggy's full weight came down on his right shoulder. 'What are you doing?'

'Trying to open the window a bit more. It's only on a little catch. Ah ... got it!' Ziggy announced as the window dropped backward into the room. 'Great. Stand still while I climb in.'

But Gonch didn't stand still. He took off up the corridor as he heard a warning shout from Robbie, who they had positioned as lookout on the corner.

Robbie darted across the corridor as well and hid behind one of the cleaners' trolleys. Gonch made a dart for the cleaners' cupboard, while Ziggy was left half in and half out of the window above Mr Griffiths' door.

His legs disappeared just in time as Mrs McCluskey came round the corner and walked on past the door on her way to the Staff room. Robbie watched her go, then came out from behind one of the cleaners' trolleys, dashed across, banged on the cleaners' door for Gonch and then across to the Caretaker's room. 'Ziggy. Ziggy. You OK?'

'Yeah,' Ziggy groaned, as he opened the door and held up the spare set of keys he had removed from the hook on the wall. 'Fell on me shoulder but I'm OK.'

'Pity it wasn't your head,' Gonch said.

'What?' Ziggy said, unsure how to take the comment.

'Wouldn't have hurt then, would it? Come on,' Gonch replied.

Ziggy took a kick at him, but Gonch was away. Robbie laughed and went after him. Ziggy closed the door and followed. Then he stopped. He'd forgotten to close the window. With a shrug he turned and went after the others. They could sort that out later. Anyway, he thought to himself, if Old Groucho Griffiths returns and finds his keys gone, the window's going to be the least of our problems.

It didn't take them long to get across to the general teaching block, charge up the stairs and start trying the keys in the door. Robbie was back as lookout on the stairs. Ziggy dragged the ladder along the corridor as Gonch worked his way round the key ring. 'Like a bloomin' jailer with all this lot,' he said to Ziggy. 'Ah . . . that's it!'

Ziggy broke into a huge grin, which rapidly disappeared as he saw Gonch dash through the door and up the stairs. 'What about the ladder?' he called. 'I can't manage it meself, soft lad!!' But it was no use. Gonch had raced on ahead.

As Gonch was dashing up the stairs, past the tank and out on to the roof, Hollo had decided to give up. He had decided Gonch was never going to turn up. He would have to try and call for help, no matter what the consequences were for being caught on the roof. He cupped his hands together and screamed, 'Help!' He then jumped back with shock as Gonch's head popped over the hole.

'OK. Give us a chance. We'll have you out in a minute!'

Then the head was gone. Hollo blinked. Had it been real? Did he really see Gonch? 'Gonch!' he shouted. No response. Hollo wasn't sure if he was imagining it. He tried again, 'Gonch, are you there?'

But Gonch wasn't. He'd dashed back across the roof and was ducking through the hatch and into the tank room when he banged his head on something that hadn't been there before. He let out a cry and looked up. It was the ladder. Ziggy and Robbie had dragged it up the stairs and were now trying to shove it through the hole.

'What are you doing?' Gonch asked, a bit annoyed by the bump.

'Waiting for the ice-cream man,' Ziggy said. 'What does it look like we're doing?'

'Who's on lookout?' Gonch demanded. Looking directly at Robbie.

'We didn't know where you'd gone!' Robbie protested.

'I went to tell Hollo we were here, didn't I, cluck brain,' Gonch fired back.

'Awright, awright,' Ziggy said. 'We won't get him out if we barney among ourselves, now, will we? Robbie. Bomb back down and keep BY.'

'What?'

'Keep lookout.'

'Oh. Why didn't you say so then.'

'I did.'

'You didn't. You said BY,' Robbie pointed out.

'It means the same,' Ziggy explained.

'Not to me it doesn't,' Robbie continued to argue.

Gonch had had enough. 'Robbie!'

'What?'

'Just do it, eh?' Gonch asked.

Robbie shrugged and moved off towards the stairs, muttering something about a stupid scouse ... but that was all he said as Ziggy splashed some water from the tank at him, shouting, 'I heard that!'

Gonch stepped in again. 'Could we just get on with saving Hollo?'

'I'm waiting for you,' Ziggy countered. Gonch took a breath, counted to ten and took one end of the ladder. 'Right. Lift your end,' he gold Ziggy. 'Now push. That's it. That's it. . . . Wait. Hold it!'

'No choice, have we,' Ziggy said. 'It's stuck.'

Sure enough. While the previous ladder was too small for the hole in the roof, this one was too big to go over the top of the tank and through the hatch. It hit the roof outside before it cleared the top of the tank. Gonch had miscalculated again. He had failed Spud Murphy once again.

'Give it a shove,' he suggested to Ziggy. Ziggy shoved. It moved on a few inches but then stuck. 'No use,' Ziggy announced. Gonch looked. Then nodded. 'OK. Pull it out.'

The two lads took hold of the ladder and tugged. It didn't move. They tugged again. It wouldn't budge. Worse than that, it was jammed in such a way that it blocked the hatch on to the roof. They couldn't get the ladder out on to the roof to help Hollo. And they couldn't even get past the ladder to tell him. They were all well and truly stuck.

FIFTEEN

While the lads were stuck in the tank room, Georgina was stuck at the bottom of the stairs. She was standing at the door where she had left Ant at lunchtime, looking across towards the main gate where she was supposed to meet him. However, she couldn't. She didn't dare step out of the building. Over at the main gate, Imelda and Helen were waiting.

Georgina decided to go back into the block. She could go to the far end and cross behind the Science Block, past the Speaking Wall and go out through the gate to the kitchens. She wouldn't be able to see Ant again, but he'd understand. She'd tell him tomorrow. There was only one thing wrong with her plan. It wouldn't work. It wouldn't work because standing behind her, was Mr Griffiths.

As she turned she bumped into him. Standing, watching her with his hands on his hips.

'And where do you think you're going to, young lady?' he asked.

'Er . . . sorry, I just wanted to go through and out the other door,' Georgina explained.

'Too late. It's locked.'

'Oh. . . . Is there any chance of unlocking it? I'd prefer to go out this way.'

'Oh, would you now?' Griffiths asked. 'No doubt you would. And where would we be if everyone did what they preferred, eh? Tell me that?'

Georgina didn't answer.

'Well, I'll tell you. In a bigger mess than we are now, young lady.'

Georgina looked across at the main gate. I couldn't be in a bigger mess, she thought. 'And you should be out there,' said Griffiths. 'On your way home. Now come on. Hop it.'

'Oh please. Is there no chance of going out the other way?' Georgina pleaded. It was no use.

'No. Now out.' Griffiths pointed to the door.

Georgina hesitated. She knew Imelda would see her as soon as she stepped out of the door. And were was Ant?

'Come on, young lady. Hurry up. Even if you haven't got a home to go to, I have.'

Georgina started to move towards the door. Mr Griffiths seemed satisfied with this and moved towards the stairs. Then he stopped. 'Oh . . . ,' he called after Georgina. She stopped. 'You haven't seen a big wooden ladder anywhere, have you?'

'Er . . . no. Sorry!'

Griffiths nodded and then went upstairs, shaking his head and muttering. He was a funny man, Georgina thought. He's so nasty to us, but he really cares about the school. Probably thinks we shouldn't be here. However, she didn't dwell on it very long as she hesitated by the door again. Watching Imelda. Oh, *where* was Ant?

Although Georgina couldn't see him, Ant was actually close by. He was standing by the corner of the general teaching block, also watching Imelda and Helen. He knew that they would be waiting for Georgina. He also knew that she was supposed to be meeting him there. If Imelda and Helen saw her they would go for her. Then he would go for them.

He had sat and thought it through during Computer Studies. Developing a reasoned, logical approach to the problem. Quite appropriate he had thought. The idea had first occurred to him when he had met Georgina and escorted her between the last two lessons of the day. They had been followed by Imelda and Helen, throwing jibes and insults at them all the way. He had been very tempted to turn and punch Imelda there and then, but Georgina had stopped him. She reminded him that he was still under threat from Bronson. If he was caught fighting it would only create more trouble. If he was caught fighting with a younger girl it would be a disaster.

Ant had listened. He took the advice and waited until Georgina was safe under the watchful stare of a member of staff before he went off to Computer Studies. As he sat listening to Mr King droning on about megabytes and drive systems, he had worked out how to deal with Imelda. As he watched Laura Reagan and Julia Glover studying Mr King for any signs of his relationship with Fay Lucas, although Ant was at a loss to know what signs there could be, he had come up with a solution. It was a bit risky. A bit rough on Georgina, but she had put up with a lot from Imelda. If it worked, it would solve the problem for good.

It was actually quite simple. He would wait until Imelda and Helen attacked Georgina. Then he would attack them. If anyone saw it he could claim, quite justifiably, that he only did it to help Georgina. They couldn't get him for that. Not even Bronson. He just had to make sure he got it right. He had to make sure he got to them before they really hurt Georgina.

SIXTEEN

While the waiting game was being played out at ground level, Hollo was having to continue with his waiting game up on the roof. He was still staring at the hole. He was still convinced he had seen Gonch. His head had popped into view. He was sure it had. Gonch had even said something about having him out in a minute. But that was ten minutes ago. He looked at his watch again. Quarter to four. Where was he now? 'Gonch!' Hollo called. 'Gonch! Are you there?'

Gonch wasn't. He was now on his way over to the Gym. After several more futile attempts to free the ladder, he and Ziggy had decided that what they needed was a rope. They couldn't get enough of a hold on the ladder to give it a really good tug. The problem was, they had to stretch across the water tank and after Gonch nearly went in for another unscheduled swim, he had decided that another course of action was necessary. Hence his dash across to the Gym. If they had a rope they could tie it on to the ladder and get a good tug to free it. They could then use the rope to haul Hollo out of the hole.

The idea was a good one and would probably have worked, until Robbie, still on lookout, spotted Mr Griffiths coming up the stairs. He jumped back and ran along towards the door to the tank room. He opened the door and shouted up to Ziggy, still trying to free the ladder, 'Watch it! Griffiths.' He then dashed on and hid in one of the classrooms.

Ziggy didn't quite catch what Robbie had shouted. He was splashing water on to the ladder, trying to see if he could lubricate it a bit and slide it out. He stood up and walked to the top of the stairs to see what Robbie wanted.

Mr Griffiths was now at the top of the stairs and pulling out his own set of keys. He was going to check the state of the water tank. He stopped when he reached the door and found it open. He looked around. He remembered locking the door. Then he tutted to himself. 'I bet it's those roof repairers. I knew I shouldn't have given them a key.' He pulled the door open and called, 'Hello? Anyone up there?' He then started up the steps.

If Robbie's heart missed a few beats, Ziggy's nearly stopped. He hadn't had such a shock since the security guard at the airport had stopped him! For an instant he was frozen to the spot. He recognised the voice instantly. Groucho Griffiths.

He looked around for somewhere to hide. There was nowhere. The room had four walls and a roof. The tank was not even in the centre. It was over to one side so you could walk around it to the hatch. And what would Groucho make of that? His ladder stuck in the hatch!

Elsewhere, Gonch was totally unaware of the impending collapse of their plan. He had a problem of his own. The Gym club was in full swing – swinging about on the ropes he had hoped to borrow to save Hollo. He was just about ready to admit defeat and call in the school staff to help his friend when he spotted something on the notice board outside the Gym. A leaflet announcing a trip. Not just any trip. A mountaineering trip. Of course – the Outward Bound Club. That lot had their own ropes, didn't they, Gonch thought. And they keep them in a separate storeroom. Off he went. If any of the sports staff had seen him not only would they have been suspicious of his speed, but they would have put him in the athletics team.

Back in the tank room Mr Griffiths was now staring, mouth open, at the ladder sticking out of the hatch. 'What the. . . .? he kept muttering. Finally, he walked round to it. He looked for evidence of life, but could find none. There was no sign of anyone. Not even Ziggy.

Mr Griffiths was now convinced. 'Those roof repairers,' he muttered. 'They were looking for a ladder to spread the load because the roof was dangerous.' He took hold of the ladder. 'They only had to ask.' He tugged. It didn't move. He tugged it again. 'I'd have let them use it,' he muttered as he tugged again. This time it came free, but toppled over into the tank. The water splashed over the side. 'Blast!' he cursed.

He then pulled the ladder out and looked into the tank. It was rusty coloured. He gave a short nod, obviously deciding that the roof repairers were no doubt responsible for discolouring the school's water. 'I'll have a few words to say to them tomorrow, and no mistake.' He was still muttering as he took the ladder down and locked the door.

At the top of the stairs he stopped and looked at himself. He was filthy. Partially from freeing the ladder, and partially from being splashed by the water. 'Dear, oh dear.' Now he was annoyed. 'No right to move it. No right at all,' he muttered as he tried to brush some of the dirt off his hands on to his overall. 'Well, I'm not taking it back. They can put it back themselves. They moved it. They can return it.'

So saying he wandered across to the toilets Ziggy and Gonch had hidden in earlier. At least he could have a quick rinse. He went in, still muttering about the roof repairers.

As Mr Griffiths disappeared, Robbie's head popped into view through the glass in the door of the classroom in which he'd been hiding. Where was old Griffiths? He came out and tried the door to the tank room. It was locked. Then he spotted the ladder. What had happened to Ziggy? Where was Gonch? Who had the keys to the door?

Robbie had no time to work out any of the answers to these questions as he heard footsteps on the stairs. Was it Gonch? No. There were too many. It sounded like three or four people. Robbie decided not to take any chances and darted back inside the classroom.

No sooner had he done so, than Laura, Julia and Calley reached the top of the stairs. 'There it is!' exclaimed Julia, pointing to the ladder.

'Well, what did you expect?' Laura asked. 'Do you think I'd forget where I ruined my tights?'

'Come on then. Quick,' Calley urged. 'You two take one end each and I'll get in the middle.'

The three girls picked up the ladder and hurried off down the stairs. As they did, Robbie popped out of the classroom once again. He crossed to the top of the stairs to watch them go. What on earth would they need that for, he wondered, but then he remembered Griffiths as he heard the sound of flushing. He dashed back to the classroom just in time, as Griffiths came out of the toilet and turned to go down the stairs. Then he stopped. He noticed the ladder was gone. It had disappeared again. He looked around, then over the railings, but the girls had gone. He crossed to the door to the tank room and tried it.

It was still locked. He stood, thinking for a moment. Something funny was going on, and he was going to find out what it was. He hurried away down the stairs.

After another moment Robbie came out again. He looked over the railings. No sign of old Griffiths. No sign of Gonch either. He went across to the door to the tank room and banged on it. 'Ziggy!' he called out. He tried again. After four times, with no response, he gave up. No sign of Ziggy either. What was going on now?

SEVENTEEN

'Oi!'

Georgina jumped. It was Mr Griffiths. She turned to see him coming down the stairs. 'I thought I told you to hop it!'

Georgina moved towards the door. Even though she was caught between the Caretaker and the evil school witch, Georgina automatically went for the open space. She couldn't get away from Mr Griffiths inside, but she might stand a chance outside.

She took a step toward the door, had a look toward the main gate where Imelda and Helen were still waiting, then took a deep breath. With a step back to pick up speed she charged the door and crashed through, running off in the same direction as she had seen Laura, Julia and Calley carrying the ladder. Away from Imelda.

Ant didn't see Georgina come out of the general teaching block, although he heard the door crash open. What alerted him to the fact that things had started to happen was Imelda. He saw her nudge Helen and then take off into the school. He knew they must be chasing Georgina, but he knew he had to wait until they had gone past him, in case they saw him. He had to catch them in the act if his plan was going to work.

If Georgina had known what Ant was planning she might not have hurt herself. But she didn't. And she cut her knee quite badly.

As soon as she came out of the general teaching

block she ran as fast as she could towards the canteen. She still hoped to outrun Imelda and escape through the gate by the kitchens. She crossed the playground and round the corner by the Speaking Wall. She couldn't remember later how it happened, although she did recall looking back over her shoulder to check where Imelda was. She fell as she turned back to face the front. Laura, Julia and Calley were there right in front of her. With that stupid ladder.

Georgina saw it too late. She tried to jump over it, but didn't make it. She remembered seeing it in front of her as she jumped. The next thing she remembered was a kick in the back and the hot breath of Imelda down her neck as someone seemed to drop a ton of bricks on her back.

Then the pain was gone. She rolled over and saw Imelda's contorted face as someone was pulling her up by the hair. Georgina shifted position. She could see Ant. She also saw Helen, rushing at him and swinging her bag. She went to cry out, but there was no need. Ant had seen Helen. Holding on to Imelda with his right hand, he lashed out with his left and slapped Helen across the face.

As Helen fell back, Laura and Julia grabbed her arms. Imelda was now trying to twist and pull herself free – her hair wasn't as long as Georgina's, so it was more difficult to hold. But again Ant had the situation under control. As Imelda twisted, he let her go and gave her shoulder a shove to propel her round even faster. As she spun, he grabbed her lapels with one hand and slapped her twice across the face with the other.

Everyone was shocked. Even Imelda. She stood stiff.

'Weren't expecting that, were you?' Ant said. 'Not used to picking on someone who'll hit you back, are you?'

It was true. Imelda wasn't used to it. She also wasn't used to being picked up by her armpits. However, she suddenly found herself lifted into the air as Ant slipped his hands from her lapels to under her arms.

'Get off, you! What are you doing?' she screamed.

'Just thought you might like to stick around for a while,' Ant said as he walked towards the Speaking Wall.

'Get off. Get off. Get off!' Imelda screamed as she realised what he was going to do. She was right.

Ant shoved her against the sticky, gooey mess that Mr Griffiths had painted on to the wall, and let her slide down to the ground, making sure she was well and truly covered. Then he knelt down beside her. 'Now you listen. I don't really care what your evil little mind gets up to. But don't – ever – bother – Georgina again. Got it?'

Imelda didn't answer.

Ant took hold of her hair with one hand and clenched his other into a fist. 'I said have you got it?'

Imelda nodded. It was an effort. But she managed it.

Ant pulled her up. 'Now disappear. Now!' He shoved her on her way. To everyone's surprise she just went. Even Imelda knew when she was beaten. Laura and Julia let Helen go as well and she sloped off after her fallen leader. As they disappeared from sight, Ant went across to Georgina, who was dabbing at her bloodied knee with a handkerchief. 'You OK, Gee?'

She looked up and smiled. 'I am now.'

Ant turned to Laura. 'Sorry about that. But . . .' he just shrugged.

'No need to apologise,' Laura grinned. 'I've been hoping someone would do that for ages.'

They all exchanged a grin as Ant looked at Georgina. 'Come on, Gee. Let's go and get a plaster on that.' He put his arm round her and they walked away.

'How . . . how did you know?' Georgina asked, resting her head on his shoulder.

'Oh . . . er . . . I just happened to see her go after you.' Ant looked down at her knee. He decided it would be best if he didn't explain how he'd managed to see it.

'I'm glad you did,' Georgina said as they too went round the corner of the Speaking Wall. She wasn't really bothered about her knee. Her problem with Imelda had been resolved. All they had to do now was practise Ant's mum's writing for the note to Bronson the next morning. Life suddenly seemed wonderfully simple.

EIGHTEEN

Meanwhile, somebody else's problems were still not resolved. Even with Ziggy lying on the roof and talking to him through the hole, Hollo was getting more and more impatient.

'Well, where is he now?' he asked Ziggy.

'I told you. He's gone for some rope.'

'Where to?'

'I don't know, do I? I've been up here, haven't I?'

He had indeed. He had the dirt to prove it. Ziggy was covered in black dust from head to toe. When Griffiths had come up the stairs, the only place he could find to hide was under the water tank. He had jumped down and squeezed beneath it. The floor was covered in years of dust, but at that particular moment Ziggy hadn't cared. All he wanted to do was avoid getting caught. His problem now would be explaining to his mum why he had left home that morning as a schoolboy to return as a coal-miner. Still, his mum was easier to deal with than Old Groucho Griffiths. Especially with his dad working nights.

Ziggy thought back to when old Griffiths had seen the ladder. He started to chuckle.

'What are you laughing about?' Hollo demanded. From where he was he couldn't see much to laugh about. He couldn't see much at all.

'Oh . . . Just thinking about old Groucho,' Ziggy told him. 'You should have seen him. He kept changing colours he was that mad. He kept going red. Then white. Then purple. He nearly went green when the ladder went in the water, and all. He was like one of them animals.'

'What animals?' Hollo asked.

'You know. Er . . . they change their skin or something to disguise themselves.'

'A chameleon?' Hollo offered.

'Yeah. That's them. Chameleon Griffiths,' Ziggy laughed. 'He must have gone about fifty shades of red.'

'Yeah. Well, it's a good job he didn't come out here, isn't it?'

'Yeah,' agreed Ziggy and looked at the hole. 'He'd have been a dead chameleon if he'd seen this.'

'We'll all be dead if Gonch has lost those keys,' Hollo moaned. 'I'll either die down here, or we'll get killed by the staff if they have to get us out.'

Ziggy wasn't really listening. He was fed up with Hollo's moaning. He wouldn't mind, but Hollo had only been in there for two hours, and Ziggy thought anyone could last that long. Ziggy remembered squashing himself under the seat of the aeroplane to Manchester for an agonising sixty minutes. Try doing that before you moan about being stuck down a hole, mate, Ziggy thought.

'What do you reckon it is, anyway. That room, like?'

Hollo didn't respond. He was in no mood for guessing games.

Ziggy was, though. 'It's . . . it's a bit like one of them secret rooms in the pyramids, isn't it? You know, where they used to bury the Pharaohs, and that. Like a sort of hidden grave.'

'I don't care,' Hollo said. 'I just don't want it to be my hidden grave.'

'Hey up!' Ziggy suddenly exclaimed and disappeared from the hole. Hollo started to worry. He remembered last time someone had appeared and then disappeared again.

'What?' he shouted.

'I'm back!' Gonch said as he poked his head over the side of the hole. 'And look,' he added, as he showed Hollo the rope. For the first time in two hours Hollo was able to smile. At last he felt there was a chance to escape.

'Hang on!' said Gonch as he stood up to face Ziggy.

'Where's Robbie?' Ziggy asked.

'On lookout again.'

'Let's get on with it then,' Ziggy suggested. 'Where'd you get the rope?'

'From the Outward Bound Room,' Gonch informed them. Then he grinned. 'With a bit of luck, we'll have Hollo out in one mighty Outward Bound!'

The others just groaned as Gonch started to let out the rope.

'Anyone see you?' Ziggy asked.

'I'm here, aren't I?' Gonch replied.

Ziggy nodded. That was true. 'How d'you get in?' Ziggy asked.

Gonch just held up Griffiths' keys. They both laughed.

'Magic!' Ziggy announced. 'Do you think we'd get away with keeping them?'

Gonch shook his head. 'No chance. There'd be a full scale alert if these went missing. Which is why we've got to get them back soon.' Ziggy nodded. That was true. Gonch grinned and added, 'But, at least we know where we can get them in future, don't we?'

They both laughed again as they lowered one end

of the rope down to Hollo. This time Gonch had done Spud Murphy proud. There was enough rope to haul Hollo up from the ground floor if necessary. He'd taken no chances this time.

'You got it, Hollo?' Gonch shouted.

'Yeah. Go on!'

Gonch and Ziggy took hold of the rope and pulled. Hollo was lifted about half a metre off the floor, but that was all. The rope jammed on the broken edge of the hole.

'We'll need Robbie,' Gonch announced.

'OK,' Ziggy responded and dashed off to get him. Within two minutes all three lads were tugging at the rope, but with no effect. It would move a little, but then jam on the broken edges of the roof timbers.

'What's happening?' Hollo shouted. He was now swinging about one metre off the floor, and becoming more worried by the minute. His fears increased as he suddenly felt himself descending again. 'What's happening? What's happening?' he shouted.

Gonch's head popped into view. 'It keeps getting stuck on the edge. The rope gets wedged in these jagged bits.'

'Can't you just pull me up to the top. I'll climb out then,' Hollo suggested.

'Too dangerous. This might break away like before. You could really hurt yourself if you fall again.'

'Well, what are you going to do?' Hollo asked.

'Think about it!' Gonch said as he pulled himself back from the hole and faced Ziggy and Robbie.

'It needs a smooth edge or something,' Robbie was saying to Ziggy.

'Yeah,' said Ziggy. 'What we need is a pole. To lay across the hole like. So we can drop the rope over it and pull him up.'

'Yeah,' Robbie nodded. 'But where are we going to get a pole from?'

'What about the Gym again?' Ziggy suggested.

Gonch nodded. They were on the right track. 'OK,' he said. 'I'll go back. I won't be a minute.' He started off towards the hatch to the tank room.

'Hurry up,' Ziggy called. 'Chameleon might come back looking for more ladders.' Gonch stopped half-way through the hatch.

'That's it. That's it!' he shouted as he headed back to the hole.

'What?' Ziggy asked.

'The ladder. There's a ladder down there.' Gonch grabbed the rope and shouted to Hollo, 'Hollo, tie the rope to the ladder.'

'Why?'

'Just do it!' Gonch ordered. Hollo did. They hoisted the ladder out. Placed it across the hole, lowered the rope over it and within thirty seconds Hollo was free.

'Almost a mighty Outward Bound!' Gonch declared. 'Yeah. And it only took you two hours,' Hollo added sarcastically.

'C'mon. Let's go,' Gonch said as he set off towards the hatch.

'What about all this stuff?' Hollo asked.

'Leave it,' Gonch called.

'But . . . but shouldn't we tell someone about the hole?' Robbie asked.

'Yeah,' said Ziggy. 'Let's leave a message.'

'Where?' asked Robbie.

'On the Speaking Wall,' stated Ziggy. 'Where else?'

NINETEEN

By the time the four steeplejacks had come down from
the roof, knocked on Mr Griffiths' door to make sure
he wasn't in before throwing the spare set of keys
through the still open window above his door, Laura,
Julia and Calley had finished the task they had set
themselves – distributing the SPEC leaflets.

'That should teach him a lesson,' Laura said.

'Yeah. Serves him right,' said Julia. 'Well done,
Calley. The leaflets look great.'

'Yes. Well done, Calley,' Laura added.

'Well, it was your idea, Laura,' Calley replied.

Laura nodded an acknowledgement and the three
girls stood back to admire their handiwork. A job
well done. She turned to Julia. 'On the way home we
could. . . .' She let it hang in the air. She knew Julia
would pick it up. She did.

'We could what?' Julia asked.

'Go down to the precinct!' Laura suggested.

'For what?'

'To get your ears pierced!' Julia looked a bit surprised. 'Come on,' encouraged Laura. 'Take a leaf
out of Ant Jones's book. Take the bull by the horns.
Just do it!'

Julia thought for a moment. 'OK, I will!'

Laura laughed. She knew Julia meant it. Until they
got down there. Then she'd chicken out again. Still,
she thought. We might catch Fay Lucas and Mr King.
They seem to spend a lot of time down there. We
might even catch them looking at engagement rings!

'What are you grinning about?' Julia asked as they walked away.

'Oh, nothing,' Laura replied. 'It'll keep.'

As the girls walked away they didn't notice four steeplejacks approach the Speaking Wall. Gonch was already shaking a spray can, even though Ziggy had tried to tell him it wouldn't work. However, he was wrong. The girls had fixed it. They all stopped when they saw the results.

'It's brilliant!' Ziggy announced. That'll really get Chameleon going, that will!' They all laughed as Gonch stepped forward and sprayed in large letters 'WHICH TEACHING BLOCK IS IN MINT CONDITION?' Hollo took the can off him and added beneath it: 'THE ONE WITH THE HOLE IN THE MIDDLE.'

'Come on,' said Robbie nervously. 'Let's go before someone comes.'

'Hang on. Just one more,' said Ziggy and took the can from Hollo, 'AND WATER TANKS DO WE GET?' he sprayed.

They all laughed and started to walk away, but Gonch, always wanting the last word, grabbed the can and went back and sprayed: 'WHY DID GROUCHO BECOME A CHAMELEON?' Then he added: 'HE SAW A LADDER MESS!' and sprayed a huge arrow pointing at the ladder the girls had left behind. The others groaned but ran as Ziggy shouted, 'Watch it. Chameleon!' They all turned to see Mr Griffiths approaching, and dashed off round the side of the Speaking Wall.

Fortunately, he didn't notice them, probably because he'd noticed a few other things. The first was the ladder. There it was again. Large as life. Exactly where he'd left it. That was puzzling enough, but not nearly so bad as the other sight. The whole wall, from top to bottom, from side to side, was covered in leaflets. They had been stuck to his gooey paint. And over the leaflets someone had already started to spray graffiti. The wall was back to square one. Almost back to the way it was! An eyesore!

As old Griffiths kicked the wall in frustration, the four lads ran out of the main gate, still laughing at the thought of Chameleon's reaction to what the girls had done to the Speaking Wall, and what they themselves had sprayed on to it.

It was only when they were down the road that Ziggy remembered he had some unfinished business. 'Bloomin' Davies!' he suddenly said.

'What?' asked Gonch.

'I said I was going to sort her out today. Once and for all,' Ziggy said as he looked back towards the school. 'Too late now,' Robbie said. 'She'll be well gone now.'

'Can't you do it tomorrow?' Hollo asked.

'Yeah ... but ... well, I wanted to do it today,' Ziggy moaned.

'Why today?' asked Gonch.

'Oh, I dunno,' muttered Ziggy as he turned away from the school and continued walking. 'She just ... she just always seems to get away with it, doesn't she? Always!'

The others nodded and followed him away. 'You can get her next time, Zig,' Robbie said.

'Yeah,' said Gonch. 'No need to be pigzig about it!'

Ziggy took a kick at him, but missed, as they walked away.

None of them noticed Ant and Georgina standing by the telephone box on the corner. None of them noticed the smiles on their faces. Imelda didn't always get away with it!

However, the four steeplejacks had only gone another few steps when Gonch suddenly stopped dead in the middle of the pavement and turned to Hollo. 'Where's me undies?' Hollo looked horrified. So did Gonch. 'You didn't . . . you didn't leave them up there?' he asked Hollo.

Hollo couldn't speak. He just nodded and started to laugh. So did the others. 'Now that,' chuckled Ziggy, 'really is something to be pigzig about.' This time it was Gonch who took a kick at Ziggy. He missed too.